ALBERTINE

to my sister Gillian Rose

Albertine

Jacqueline Rose

Chatto & Windus

LONDON

Published by Chatto & Windus 2001

2 4 6 8 10 9 7 5 3 1

Copyright © Jacqueline Rose 2001

First published in Great Britain in 2001 by
Chatto & Windus
Random House, 20 Vauxhall Bridge Road,
London SW1V 2SA

Random House Australia (Pty) Limited
20 Alfred Street, Milsons Point, Sydney,
New South Wales 2061, Australia

Random House New Zealand Limited
18 Poland Road, Glenfield,
Auckland 10, New Zealand

Random House (Pty) Limited
Endulini, 5A Jubilee Road, Parktown 2193, South Africa

The Random House Group Limited Reg. No. 954009
www.randomhouse.co.uk

A CIP catalogue record for this book
is available from the British Library

ISBN 0 7011 6976 1

Papers used by Random House are natural,
recyclable products made from wood grown in sustainable forests;
the manufacturing processes conform to the environmental
regulations of the country of origin

Typeset by Deltatype Ltd, Birkenhead
Printed and bound in Great Britain by
Biddles Ltd, Guildford and King's Lynn

The Tomb of Albertine lies next to my cradle.

Marceline Desbordes-Valmore

The pages I would write, Albertine, above all the Albertine of then, would certainly not have understood . . . Had she been capable of understanding them, she would, for that very reason, not have inspired them.

Marcel Proust

PART ONE

IF YOU open the windows, you can feel the air move at once. Slowly it pushes its way through the gap, down the frame and into the room. The air is heavy, but gathers speed as if collecting itself for a struggle. For a second I can breathe. I can feel its presence as a type of freedom. But almost before the breeze has reached me it starts pressing under the door. Forced by the pull of its own current, it will be making its way down the corridor to where he waits, suffering his thoughts of me.

I have never opened the windows before and I know he will hear and read its deadly message. There is perhaps nothing so hard to imagine, for someone who has never known asthma, as the idea that air can suffocate. That it does not free but constrains, grips the throat, makes each fibre convulse, hammers the whole body with its blows. Maybe that's why I did it so loudly, made such a fanfare out of my rage. As much because I don't really believe that it can kill him, as because I do.

When I first entered this house, it had the wonder of something you never dare to believe. It felt as if I were breaking in, crossing a sacred threshold, scaling the walls. I knew I was way out of my class. A home is not something I could ever feel at ease in. We have that much in common, straining through our mothers, although in different ways. He because, even when she is away, she is also here, never releasing her hold. I because, with consequences that are at times strangely similar, I never knew mine. I have had the luxury of being lost. It has allowed me to cast my net wide. He, spoilt for stability and privilege, has contracted his forces, whittled down his strength. Huddled inside the panic of his safety, he draws others into the space of his fragile bodily compass and the unrelenting remit of his mind.

On the first day we met, he did not know I could see him. His amazement bubbled around him, he looked like someone in a cloud. His eyes expanded towards us, his body shrank. As we swayed, girls together along the beach, nothing could touch us. If we took such pleasure in each other's company, it was because we were so confident that, unless we first chanced it, no one else would dare. The tremors that passed between us, fine threads running one to the other, limb to limb, were for our delight alone. Although our bodies were calling, 'Look at us,' we weren't really asking to be seen. Maybe that's why his answering excitement, which rushed in our direction, halted before us, as if it had already collided with a wall of future pain.

At first his pleasures were as fleeting and chancy as ours. Nothing can compromise you or get ugly if you never let attachment get a grip. How could it, if contact is for its own sake alone? Every gesture was gratifying, cocooned in its own spoils. Even on the rare days when, under an unbroken sky, the glare was constant, we took our cue from the sea. Day in, day out, we would watch the water creep up, run its fingers along the front and then pull away from the shore. In my little group, we were as resourceful as our curiosity. It was our only possession. But, unlike other possessions, there was no point in trying – that would have ruined it – to keep it all in one place. When I first moved towards him the thrill was in the lightness. With a puzzled innocence which drew us, he asked to join in one of our games. As I skirted against him, his body trembled and contracted. It was not just his frailty but also the sheer freedom, which gave me the impression, as strange as it was overwhelming, that there wasn't anybody there.

Today I think that to be young and on the turn gives a unique vision which we should hold on to for as long as we can. Inside that riotous muddle you cannot believe that your body is matched to your mind. You may as well throw yourself to the wind. Looking back on that moment, I am struck by its peculiar, lurching grace. We were all greed and clamour, hungry bodies with our eyes on the stars. We liked to tantalise our audience without ever letting them in on our dreams. We delighted in being provocative, but the people we provoked, the ones we most surprised, were ourselves.

Perhaps such provocation is too much to endure. Certainly, as this story will tell, it didn't last. Although I am determined to have one more try. Not to become the person I was, but one taste or slip of her is all it will take, I am sure, to call her back out and usher her forwards on her path. Everything from those early days, everything that has happened since, makes me believe I owe it to myself. And to him. Perhaps we trapped each other as a way of bringing our own excitement to heel. Perhaps the torment of this past year has been our shared answer to a life left gaping, too threatening finally, less opportunity, more like an endlessly repeated tease. I have always been a tease. Cruel – he saw that at once. But also as a call on the world to keep its promise open. For me, to be reckless was no brief and innocent freedom, a deal struck, as they say, before settling down. Innocence had nothing to do with it; it was rather a case of premonition, or panic before its time. I think I have always known that, given half a chance, the love which binds – the one girls are meant to go out of their way to secure – can be the most deranging of them all.

This is also, it is true, the story of a girl who wanted to marry. I wanted to feel that I'd arrived. Being out on a limb, I had discovered, promises more than it yields. Socially, it started to feel that the world was shrinking under the same pulse which made it so exhilarating, the same energy which, deep inside me, allowed it to stretch and swim. He knew, more than anybody, that if you look closely at someone you have only seen at a distance their contours start to shift. They become somebody else and you lose the very thing which made you want to get close. Bestow on anyone the gift or shape of your concentration and you miss them even before you begin. But I don't think he has ever quite understood – why should he? his class and sex have protected him – the disaster which followed, above all for me, from the drama he so brilliantly staged in defiance of that principle, as his way of putting it to the test. I would be as close as you can get, but the thrill would never go away. What neither of us realised was that to succeed in such a task, with the best love in the world, would be hateful. We have been wrapped in a membrane thin to bursting, even if its fabric is this house's ancient and more than solid walls. Mostly it has felt like living with someone trying to expel the air out of a balloon. Has he ever realised, I sometimes wonder, how much his conditions of living and loving, far more than his illness, have made it impossible for either one of us to breathe?

—

When I first opened my mouth in his company I think he was truly shocked. My little group of the shore revelled in the spirit of a talk which we had ripped from the streets. Heaven knows where he thought I was from. At the Normandy seaside, where he spent every summer, we were birds of passage hovering in the vicinity, while he was the resident of that most famous and glorious of retreats. The Grand Hotel de la Plage spread along the beach which for it named itself, with no regard for any of the smaller, greyer establishments which braced themselves at either end against its bulk. All along the front façade arched windows gazed at the horizon, like a duchess raising an eyebrow at some affront. From whatever angle you looked the hotel always seemed to be staring at the sea. Apart from the carriages which deposited their illustrious guests at the rear entrance, nothing on the other side, beyond a sweeping avenue appearing to curve out of nowhere, was allowed to exist. Not the old fishing town, from which daily the hotel drew all its supplies and its servants, who disappeared at points in the night like waves retreating from the shore. Not the small villages set just a few miles away from the centre, with their clusters of rented houses for those wanting their small share of the season, brown and grey stone bleached bare by the wind. Here it was that, for the summer months of the year, my aunt and I, and most of my girlfriends and their families, lived. But it was not where we chose to spend our time. Except at the end of the day when together, Andrée,

Gisèle, Rosamonde and I, slowing our pace from the frolics of the afternoon, would find a way of bringing in the dark.

In Normandy it is almost always windy. Everything moves, apart from the Grand Hotel – the waves falling like old men on to the sand, the flags of the casino hitting the side of the poles, the hotel awnings closing down their shade needlessly against a grey sky. As we rode along the front on our bicycles, our skirts billowing up against the wheels, I could feel the wind coil itself around my ankles, flushing out my cheeks, slapping raw against my eyes. Our cries, like those of the seagulls circling above our heads, went screeching out with the tide. I always liked to think – and not only when he was watching – that the wind was picking on me.

For days on end he stared. His black hair plastered against his brow, his white features a little shocked, as if, almost ghostlike, he had been alarmed by a sudden vision of himself. But however frail, however set upon, he always seemed to belong to the place, or rather as if the whole place belonged to him. Even on the days, often the warmest, when he could be seen huddling fast against himself, like a limpet some cruel child was trying to prise away from its rock. For us, just being there at the beach, within sight of that oh-so-grand hotel, gave us a certain cachet. As we raced up and down the esplanade on our bicycles, we cocked a hoop at its magnificence while rubbing our handlebars so they would shine all the brighter from its dross. But sometime, around the third chance encounter, I started to return his stare. Then I would nudge Andrée to make her turn and look too. We were a threesome from the start. I wanted her to see him watching me. I wanted her reassurance and protection, but

I also wanted her to be part of the dare. There is perhaps nothing as exciting as a danger which you increase, make even more intense, by the very same gesture with which you ward it off. From that first moment, our tightly gathering triangle took up its positions. We had already invested our pleasure in our fears.

I could see him trying to work out our attachments. I was told later that his first guess was that we belonged, the whole troupe of us, to the racing cyclists, sporting heroes, staying at his hotel. Fast girls who couldn't possibly be racing their own race. But even this misjudgement spoke volumes of what was to come. It was our speed that drew him. With no body to speak of, he wanted to make our force his own. But only by proxy. If it was to be his possession, it was also something to be shared. Like for like, he handed us over in his mind to the men who most crudely – all for glory – mirrored our own pace. Thus quietly, invisibly, his dream of ownership, like all such dreams, set about sabotaging itself. In a way, it was a bizarre form of generosity. I don't think he has ever once seen me or enjoyed me without bringing someone else along, coupling me inside his head.

We liked best to career around the hotel. Only its stuffiness gave our licence its due. Because we were not part of his world, there was – or so it seemed to us – no end to the liberties we could take. Whenever we spun into view, rows of dowagers could be relied on to appear as if from nowhere, frowning and shaking their heads. There they would sit, backs propped, parasols at arms' length, with their lace cuffs trailing over the handles, digging the ends into the floor. A set of deckchairs shocked to find themselves all of a sudden disposable and folded away against the walls.

9

We loved the low mutters of disapproval. We would choke back our laughter while pretending to be oblivious, as we watched someone we had barely skirted pull in their chest and stuff their chins down into their throat. It was their gesture, not ours, which did the greatest violence to their self-possession. Their anger, not our carelessness, which took their breath away. Even when we were admonished, and for a brief while reined ourselves back, it still felt to us that they were the ones who had been cautioned. Straitened by their own rigidity. Whereas with no cost to our exuberance we would defer and then, as soon as the coast was clear, carry on exactly as before.

In the midst of them one morning, perfectly poised underneath the awning of the bandstand, a solitary old man, his yachting cap pressed against his ears, a few stray white hairs curling up at the back behind the rim, looked like an old fish deposited among a cackle of birds. He stared to either side of him, past the congregation and up and down the front, either taking in the new delights of being one among the ladies, or else desperate to catch sight of whoever had left him so incongruously to himself. With a flying leap, Rosamonde, red hair streaming, brown eyes standing out bright from the whites of her eyes, ran along the top of the bandstand and jumped to the ground over the old man's head. Her skirts crackled in her hand. Eyes lifted and breath held, we pressed on the balls of our feet and, miming her in perfect communion, raised ourselves one after the other on our toes. Just brushing the top of his head, she landed perfectly – heels together, toes splayed like a ballerina – at his feet. As she stood in front of him, still clutching her skirt above her ankles, he looked at her with a mixture of fury and self-reproach. As though all the lost chances of his life had just flashed before his eyes, mowing down the principles with which, up to that moment, he had so sagely resisted them. If only he had looked up as she flew! He shook his head. All the dowagers nodded. Always in search of a reason to hate us, they were congratulating themselves. He adjusted his stick, letting his weight fall on it for comfort and, shaking almost imperceptibly, his face just a shade redder, he pulled himself up before slipping, as one drowning, back into his chair.

Further down the esplanade our new friend stood watching. Only when I saw the shock rending his features did I realise that, like a servant girl on a day out at the races, I had been shrieking at the top of my voice: 'Go! Go! Go!'

—

I am very good at leaving home. I first did it before I can remember, at a time when you could say that I had no choice. I have never been told the story of what came before. There has been a hush over my life, filled with the bustle and banter of those who meant well. My aunt is one of those people who clearly believe that clutter and chatter will amply deck out any existence, even one drained, as mine was before it started, at the core. I cannot remember a time when I could not hear her voice. From the time when I could barely walk and talk, my childhood seems to have been spent on trains. Rattling carriages and rugs piled all over me − a little bundle tucked away in a corner, I must have looked like an abandoned child. Or in drawing rooms which felt like stations, points to alight at in an unstoppable journey from which we had been allowed for a moment to rest. My uncle is a diplomat. He kept travelling − his duties required it. But he also apparently believed that by speeding things up even more than necessary he could impress upon those he was serving and anyone else who cared to notice that this was not the life he would have wished upon himself. Perhaps that is why, when I try to think back, it is always my aunt whom I see. He was too quick. Dashing in and out on the pretext of some urgent business, documents flapping, as if his country's future depended on him, he looked like an overstretched waiter, platter in hand, pushing his way with his hips through swing doors. I sat quietly watching in rooms which filled with talk, mouths opening and shutting like flies above my head. When I was very young, before I could even speak, my uncle was at the embassy in Vienna. All I can remember are the sounds of a language harsh and clipped and clean – no words flushed, mouths stung and ripe as in French – bodies sucked back against the teeth.

I have never mastered the art of social conversation. In the world in which we circulate, the one whose highest echelons my friend penetrates with such ease and to which I have always aspired, talk is all. For me talking is either words gliding around to no purpose, a way of meeting nobody, not any other person, most surely not yourself. Or else it is whispering in the dark. A prelude to things unspeakable, not intended for the brim and din of the air. If I have stayed here as long as I have, it must be because part of me relishes the night which he has so masterfully closed over this house. I never know if the pleasure I take in darkness stems from the licence it offers, or whether it is the secrecy I cherish, the way it echoes the awful quiet of a world grown shameful, first because there was silence and then because there were too many words. 'What's the matter, Albertine?' 'Oh dear, everyone thinks I am happy!' 'Smile, Albertine, keep smiling,' my aunt mutters in a choked whisper, trying to cough me back down into her throat, 'It will keep the wolves from the door.'

I must admit that I have made her behaviour worse. We have been bad for each other. You only have to watch her glide into a room, scanning it for the person she is most frantic to pump and prime. Her body swells to all corners. She is pure breath and excitement. But almost before you have got the measure of her vast reach, which is truly impressive, it starts to look as if she is flailing, drowning – and bringing everyone down with her – in the expanse of her own greed. She is simply too keen. All for my sake, of course. I was to coil myself round Parisian society and together we would spiral our way to the top. He was to be catch and then bait. If I won him, the whole world would fall plump within her grasp. So there is a fine irony in the fact that, superficially at least, you might conclude that it is he who has trapped me.

Sometimes I would copy her. Her way of belonging and yet being so out of place. Then it would seem as if I had suddenly found my own tongue. In fact, whenever I spoke in her presence in public, my sense of triumph was always immediately soiled with regret. It was because I couldn't bear her pretension that, still almost a child, I would cut so brutal a swathe through the pretensions of everyone else. What matters above all in these gatherings is that everyone keep their hands clean. So when, in the course of one of her most finely cultivated tea parties, the visiting wife of the Minister of Finance declared her ignorance of kitchens, I pitched in with short-lived but exquisite pleasure, 'Surely, madame, your father was a scullion?' And then sat there watching as my words spread like a stain across the floor. I got it all from her, of course, the things I heard her say. But I was very choosy, sifting in my own fashion through the baggage of the drawing room. It was, in those early days, the only way I could find to detach myself from the pointed aim of her refinement. I had all the venom with none of the skills, none of the bared-teeth grimaces which pass for a greeting and which in the normal course of things allow, without anyone daring to notice or comment, the worst barbs to pass.

My aunt has never wanted to touch me. She stretches her arms out to all and sundry, but manages at the same time to look, at least to me, like a snake in recoil. At the slightest hint of rejection or hostility she is ready to lash out in despair. If I have been the one to register it most acutely, it is not just because in private I have heard the counterpoint, watched her rant and rail. It is also because I have always known that what most passionately fuelled her enthusiasms, the reason she embraced the world with such anguished attention, was to be rid of me. There is something about the world of diplomacy, even more for the wife of a diplomat like her, which means that you can never be present on your own terms. It is neither expected nor required. You are simply a conduit which allows other people to move through you and pass by. You may receive their impress, but it makes absolutely no difference to where you stand. Riches did not cling to us, they slid past. We went everywhere that mattered, but we were never sought. Of course, none of it was my doing, but my being an orphan fleshed out to the world what was most pitiful about her own status. I provided the perfect, dazzling, pretext for her resentment.

I think she never forgave me for the fact that, independently of her although with no increase whatso-ever in my prospects of marriage, I nonetheless started to find my own way. I started to be courted by those who found me classy because I was strange. They liked to use me as the occasion for their benevolence and good grace. It made them feel kind. But I also intrigued them. It was like being at a party of people who had come to the collective but unspoken decision to greet a whiff of something not quite wholesome as if it were a breath of fresh air.

'My aunt is my aunt,' I said to him very early in our conversations, 'but that doesn't mean I have to like her.' Is it surprising that, while I may be in my element out of doors, my greatest pleasures have been furtive? That I have always been on the lookout for those with a secret to share? Even if my search for the illicit sends me straight into the arms of what I am most eager to escape. I have never known pleasure without conjuring up on its horizon a barrier of invisible constraint. For me depravity in the bedroom is a way of flaunting my own losses, of setting them to work on my behalf. I may have been a deprived child, but I have learnt how to turn the numbing refusals of the world into my property and my vice. One of the things I have in common with him – perhaps it was the grounds of our complicity – is that I too like to devise ways of enjoying myself which nobody, not even myself in the throes of it, can see.

To say that he started to join in our little band by the shore would not be right. But then neither did he follow us around. As I think about it now, I cannot recapture exactly how he managed to make himself, slowly, surreptitiously, part of our group. We were very clear about our rules. 'Girls go about with other girls; they're not meant to have gentlemen friends.' Propriety was our cover, but it was also how we made our world safe. So, if

15

he made his way in, it must be because he, or we, subtly shifted the rules of the game. We liked his class. And I know that from the first moments, in deference both to my aunt and to my history, being in his presence raised my ambition to a pitch. But that can't explain how he seemed to manage the impossible and become one of us. I think now it was the peculiar quality of his attention. He didn't just want to possess us. He wanted to know us. Even if it meant risking his selfhood, leading his body astray, he wanted to get under our skins.

Gradually I started to realise that he was picking me out. It was hard to be sure at first because he spread himself so finely among us all, turning to this one and that, like a searchlight sweeping along a cliff. But something had happened to the relationships between us. We were not rivals for his affection, at least not to begin with. If anything, it felt as if he wanted to weave us more closely together. Because that was how he had first chanced upon us and how he liked us, but also so that his presence could slide almost without notice into the group. It was not just because there was something so girl-like about him that it seemed as if he was shifting his colours to match ours. It made it all the harder – indeed I am still not wholly convinced – to point to him as the cause of the trouble when, gradually, painfully, we started to fall apart.

Perhaps in those early days he was as interested in Andrée as me. Or even more. She is more respectable, I cannot deny, carrying no scent of scandal in her wake. Unlike me, she never has to try. He would take his place amongst us, like a latecomer at the theatre clearing his throat and mouthing silent apologies as he slips into his seat. Then, moving his head from side to side as he weighed his options, he turned into a society lady watching a tennis match through her lorgnette. His dilemma obviously carried the greatest charm. I wasn't having it. Sitting on a rock above the beach one day, I shrieked to the girls, 'Don't look! Don't look' – making sure of course that we were all in it together – and scribbled him a note, 'I really like you. Don't you see?'

He started talking to Andrée about me, reeling off compliments which she dutifully conveyed, night after night, to my room. She thought they were genuine, regardless of how carefully he studied and planned their effects. 'He means it, every word.' 'So you say,' I replied. Neither of us was giving anything away. She sat on my bed, legs curled underneath her, stroking the back of my hand, her full brown hair shading the grey of her eyes. I have always trusted Andrée. I have watched her judgements grow, her thoughts follow and gradually gain on each other like the slow-moving curves on the back of a centipede. But how cleverly he saw to it that she would make herself his emissary, and how willingly she played her part. That was what was so strange. That he could be so overcome and so calculating, so measured, at the same time. He painted me with a brush so vivid and with so fine a rhetorical flourish that it was impossible not to believe. Today I can see that he was trying, against some internal odds, to convince himself. And since neither he nor I was ever really sure, we would go increasingly in search of persuasion.

'Every detail. It's like being back at school, in one of those art classes where we had to copy every vein, rib, lobe of a leaf.' For now I was flattered. He was really looking. But I was also concerned. Never before had Andrée appeared to be examining me. She tucked her legs more firmly underneath her and shuffled closer. Then

17

lifting my hand – he made much of my hands, she told me – she pressed the ends of my fingers between her teeth.

He never seemed to consider that, by drawing Andrée into his gamble, he was increasing not only his own but her desire. It never seemed to cross his mind that he was putting new ideas into our heads. Ever since the first day he had found us at the beach, he had loved and nourished our attachment to each other on condition that it remained pure poetry, a lyric to which it would be his gift and privilege to be the most highly attuned. He was always proper. He seemed to think anything cruder would have demeaned us, all three. But it was his self-control that excited us. We were left to plot, and then perform, the carnal subtext of his restraint. We discovered a new form of curiosity and a new licence – to explore through each other what it was about us that could possibly rouse a man's desire. Up to that point the delight we took in each other had been no less passionate but all our own. There was no need for it to be fierce or possessive because no one else had any interest or stake in it. Nobody was looking in. Now suddenly it was as if someone had set up an hourglass in the room and we began to take stock of our pleasures. Wrapped around each other, we would lie talking about him. We were exhilarated and weary as before, except now we were also intrigued. What used to be a fatigue as smooth as it was impermeable to the outside world had acquired an extra skin. Without question our company had grown.

It was a Friday afternoon late in August, damp and sultry, the air heavy. The sea breeze came halfway towards us and then seemed to be towed away. We were left, the three of us in the thickness of the day – Andrée and him and me. I don't think he was that ill, not then, so our sense of being dragged through something against our best will and purpose must have come from somewhere else. In any case I know I felt it fully as much as he did. And I know that we were already sharing something, passing it round between us, not quite frantically but with a fierce determination that no one of us should be landed with it, so that whatever was going on, however discomfiting, must never be allowed to stop. Our physical gestures were as they had come to be, fleet and playful. He was caressing the back of my neck, while I was running my fingers and letting them catch in her hair.

He wanted to know when we were leaving. The season was drifting to a close. Since he so dreaded the slightest change in his circumstances, he was trying to find something he could hold on to to the last. At the time, although I was still as it seemed his prime object, the terms of his courtship meant that he had also turned his attention to her. So it wasn't immediately clear to whom the question was addressed. We pulled away and looked at each other to see which of us would answer first. Since we gained no guidance from each other's confusion, we replied in one voice. And then muffled our amazement – although it is not clear who would have been betrayed had we revealed it. We had contradicted each other, and even worse – it was the first thin crack between us – had each spurted out exactly the opposite of what the other had guessed. 'At least another month.' 'No longer than two weeks.' 'Then I will see you every other day,' he said to me. 'And you daily. To be fair to you both.' So the one who had offered more was to be portioned. And the one who had hurried forward her departure would not, for as long as she was still within reach, be allowed to get away.

But how he read us! For I had indeed hoped, by making myself more present, to reduce the heat of his expectation. Just as she had wanted to fan the flames by bringing the finale close. Effortlessly he had shut us inside our unspoken gambits and today I can only admire his talent. It set the pattern to come. Like a hidden alternator, he would break and reconnect the circuit, bringing one pair together, then, closing the shutter, block the one in front of him and open the conduit to the third. When it finally surfaced, his jealousy would be the product of his own craft. But in these early days what he knew best was how to make us restless, embarrassed by our eagerness, whether for less or for more.

I think it was that day, or perhaps the day after, that I invited him to my room. My aunt drifted in and out of the season, mainly leaving me to my own devices. But on this day she summoned me on one of her ventures. Before the evening was upon us, she had swept into the villa and gathered up everything she thought we both required. Not for the first time I had the impression that I belonged inside her suitcase. A former lady-in-waiting to a noble-woman from southern France, whom she had encoun-tered on one of her journeys with my uncle, had just married into the solid upper ranks of the Parisian bourgeoisie. The kind of progress my aunt most admired and an example for me. In the past she had always dismissed her as frivolous – insufficiently obsequious in her attendance on her mistress and far too flighty with everybody else. But now things had turned around and we were to return to the city without delay. As though she feared – thereby defeating her own purpose – that her friend's new-found status might at any moment disappear.

I had to be up at the crack of dawn and didn't want to

disturb my friends so early. We had been basking in her absence, Gisèle, Rosamonde, Andrée and I. Taking our nights slowly and never making our appearance until well into the following afternoon. We would blow on the embers of the evening to keep them alive until long after the dawn. Rushing for a train in the morning would have spoilt the luxury of a rhythm which relied on all of us keeping time. So I asked my aunt to book me into the hotel for a night. It was one of those things she could easily afford, and was indeed happy to grant me, since it gave her a grandiose sense of her own powers. Not for one moment did she suspect. I was determined to seduce him. Soiling my future was to be my avenue out of her absurdities. It would have the twin advantage of satisfying my curiosity and of ruining her carefully nursed plans.

I made my entrance into the hotel thrilled at no longer being confined to its public space. As for those who now had to serve me, I wanted them to remember me acutely while having to feign complete ignorance of my previous role. I loved the height of it. Our games had been all length and breadth. I think we felt that if we played things that way, spread ourselves horizontally, we could ignore the finely graded elevations which were the hotel's foundation and reason for being, the grounds on which it stood. I don't think I had ever looked up before. All around the lobby rose vast pillars of alabaster and marble crowned with gold-encrusted foliage, riches out of reach and hoarded uselessly at the top. The main staircase poured its carpet of roses from floor to floor before, halfway between the lower landing and the ground level, swelling out on either side like a pregnant frog. Even I could see that no one was quite meant to walk up this staircase. Like the three ladies in white crinolines, skirts swishing from step to step as I entered the lobby, three black-suited monocled gentlemen bending one step behind them in attendance, you had to be grand enough and high enough to make your descent. As I travelled up in the lift I felt the awe of someone suddenly elevated, who once, in another life, had been confined below stairs. I had never been level with the lights – all drooping crystal, scattering the currents which pulsed mechanically into the fragments of the glass. I wanted to stroke all the surfaces. Shamelessly they seemed to be reaching out to me for a response. I was so enraptured by the plushness that it took a while before I started to feel it closing in.

But, I thought, if my little band had been with me, we would swing out from the landing, wrap our legs around the white torsos of the pillars, and – to gasps of amazement or even applause, it would not be us who broke the silence – slide to the floor. It was a circus, after all.

My room was at the end of a corridor which went on so long it was as if, politely but firmly, I was being led back out on to the beach. When I finally arrived the room was dimmed with a grey-blue light, broken only by the sway of the curtains casting their shadow across the reflection of the sea. Everything looked as if it was moving. Red velvet, damask, mahogany gripped fast on to the walls and furnishings, but however much they boasted their solidity, they were powerless against the currents lifted into the room from the outside air. I knew that the proper response was not to be awed by the history on display but rather to run it back, without effort, into your own past. For as long as I stayed in this room, regardless of who I was before I entered, its lineage became mine. I couldn't be an interloper even if I tried. It was as if someone, without consulting you, had opened up a piece of costly litigation on your behalf. Only the sounds and the movement of the light, flickering at the far end of the room, stopped me from turning right around and walking back out through the door.

I laid out my few possessions and started to prepare for his visit, threw my pink satin dressing gown, with the fringe of its belt dangling, over the screen at the end of the bed, a half-undone corset, a silk stocking, my white-laced bodice, here and there, like confetti scattered incongruously by the bride. I had told him exactly at what time he should come. And also that he should tell absolutely nobody else. I was aware that this would mean some subterfuge on his part, since he had already been resident so long at this hotel that his every move and preference, in order to be properly catered for, had to be known in advance. I wanted the secrecy, but it was also my way of increasing our excitement before he so much as walked through the door.

I had suggested that he come at a time when I had already retired to bed. Resting and at his disposal – although I had used the excuse of a cold to explain why I had to have dinner, for which I had invited him to join me, in recline. I had often imagined such a scenario and gone to extraordinary lengths to produce reasons beyond my willpower as to why, against my upbringing and better judgement, I was so deliciously about to lapse. Something had to have happened which compelled me towards some small violation of the rules, making possible everything to come. I could happily avert any sense of transgression by turning it into a pressure I had to grapple with and of which I was innocent because it came from outside. As a child I had often pictured myself being captured and carried off. But not, as you might too readily assume, because I wanted to be ravished. Far from it. What looked like submission was camouflage. It was my way of concealing the true nature of an experience to be brought on at my bidding alone.

I loosened my hair in the way he had told me he liked it. When I played around on the beach or in the grounds it often became unclasped and I had always enjoyed its touch on my shoulders and neck. So far his delight concurred with my freedom. Even if the others mocked my display. Even if they already felt that my flagrancy was being too generously shared. As I sat waiting in my bed, I turned its dark curls in my fingers, letting them slip through the crevices, then wound them tighter and let go. I liked the contrast. I liked the softness as they slipped between the joints and then the tautness of my own pull. I was practising – unaware that the one thing that you cannot rehearse is a pleasure. Not, that is, if you have in mind to share it with somebody else. There was a whole world to cross, as I was to discover, between my indolent, self-caressing gesture and the games that were about to begin.

He came into the room holding an ebony stick I had never seen before, and stopped, one hand to his moustache, with his chin a fraction in the air. This was his territory and his home. He belonged. His awareness of the fact that I didn't gave him a certain arrogance, but it was slight and immediately tempered by his concern. He would protect me, not from himself, but from everything oppressive about the social charade you became part of once you officially or properly entered this hotel. He always had the finest sense of our social inequality, hoping to find a way of redeeming my relative poverty without rubbing it in. But if he looked confident he also looked almost aghast. Something extra had drained from the customary pallor of his face. His black hair, normally boyish, was pressed hard against his temple, small beads of moisture were barely visible at the top of his brow. Everything else – his mouth, his cheeks – had gone dry and white at their own heat. It was as though his daring – and up to that point it had never occurred to me that he too might have something to dare – excited but also appalled him. He seemed to be asking, 'What on earth are we doing here? Is this the only way for us to endanger what we both hate most?' All at once, our setting started to feel like an insult. It made a mockery of what was finest about our ambitions, of the best plans that we had unconsciously formed for each other: to use the other as a means of pulling ourselves away – for me from a social, and for him from a no less constant, physical distress.

You might want to say that ours was just about as conventional an arrangement between a man and woman as could be. She hands over her favours in return for his prestige. But ours was no ordinary situation. It was in the nature of his body and my status dramatically to raise the stakes. Even in the normal course of events, when such accommodations are expected although largely unspoken, there is a risk. In every encounter – however fumbling, however graced – the woman must sweep away the phantom of failure; while the more he hastens to raise her standing and deflects her from her class, the more he shows his revulsion at what she is struggling to leave behind. What infinite potential for humiliation! In our case it was made richer by his frailty and by my history, which disappeared beyond any strata into the unknown. I was so much the bolder only because I was already so demeaned. Not that it is easy for a woman to wrap herself around the body of a man as he stoops.

How could anyone ever succeed at such a task? Is that why they say that lovers are reborn? And why passion is so urgent and so brief? Because it has to gamble everything against the relics of its own past. Not just allaying, but pretending that there was never anything to fear. What kind of conjuring act is this? It was to be our peculiar magic to chart the agonies of such spurious arrangements. In my stronger moments I like to think it was a mark of our quality. We were to be granted our desires, but inside out. What we sought to leave behind would drive us so hard that it would never disappear. Instead it would show up as our unwelcome but devoted companion. He would raise me to the stars and then shut out the lights, like a master of ceremonies who suddenly decides to stop his own show, or turn his players and audience blind. And I would please him beyond his wildest dreams. But the more I did so the more I became his tormentor, body and soul.

All this is clear to me now, but even had I seen it then I am not sure that things would have turned out any differently. It was a delusion of his – it fuelled his intensity – to believe that understanding is the same as changing or redeeming yourself. So even though I can see it now, I still wish I could go back to the beginning, to those first moments in the room when what overpowered me, alongside the fraught nature of his attention, was the joy he took from being so intimately and unexpectedly in my presence. I could see the relish in his eyes, the way he noted my negligent hair, his reluctant excitement at the fall of my nightclothes, all creases and openings, over my skin. His response played beautifully to my tune. There could be no danger, not now, not ever, because his delight felt beckoned and prepared.

We hardly talked. In fact I cannot remember a word that we said, since what followed came so unremitting and so fast. He moved towards me and sat on the edge of the bed, looking at me as if our lives depended on it. I had never been that close, never been alone with him before. I had never felt him breathing. I had never had the occasion – there had always been too much noise and mental clutter – to watch the rise and fall of his chest. You are not alive unless you are moving, even if imperceptibly to yourself and others, all the time. You are not alive unless your heart is pumping the air through your lungs without fail. Increase the pace and it is not always obvious if someone is more alive or less. Why do we talk of bodies being transported? Do we ever ask ourselves how or where they are supposed to stop? As he caught his breath, I had no way of telling whether I was to be the occasion for his utmost fulfilment or distress. Just for a second, the danger and the passion circled round me before returning to their own place. I knew they had been for me, but it was unclear what he had wanted me to do with them, whether I was meant to excite him or haul him back. Such a question was not one I was expecting to have to put to myself. I was not expecting to have to think at all. As his face came towards me I could barely see it, except to register a look as ecstatic as it was remote. The closer he got to me the further he appeared to be travelling from himself. It crossed my mind with the speed of light that I was being summoned to an embrace in which at least one of us was to be lost. I was frightened not because I was vulnerable or in his power, although in one sense both these were of course true. The terror came from what he was letting me see. Later I would discover that, in his eyes, it was the risk which empowered him. It made him feel that, with nothing more to play for, the universe was in his hands. But for me at that moment, it was like looking into a crystal ball and watching yourself die.

As he flung himself towards me, I moved my head to one side of the pillow. If he landed it would not be on the softness of my face. You cannot, I am told, smother yourself. Almost falling, he reached out, so as to steady himself, for the arm which I had started to raise above my head. And then – recognising my purpose – he watched disbelieving while I pulled as hard on the bell cord as I could. We both froze. First shrill, and then duller and duller, the sound travelled – carrying me with it – through the thickness of the walls and out into the big wide world of the hotel.

We had had the unlikely experience of breath mingling without the accompanying embrace. Against all the evidence of the senses – since I am not sure we even touched – all I wanted was to pull us apart. As soon as I rang the bell he made to leave the room. But he did not believe it. He knew, as I did, that there could be no such conclusion except according to a set of rules which we had already irrevocably broken even if, to an innocent eye, it might appear that nothing had taken place. I had tried to fall back on etiquette, but neither of us was fooled. It would make no difference at our next meeting when I told him, flaunting my best outrage, that he was never to try again. It was my futile attempt to pretend that nothing, bar a misunderstood flirtation, a boy who tried to go too far, had happened. But I was sure there would be a sequel. I knew that we now belonged together. Never before had I felt so solicitous – both for myself and another – and so aroused. What had passed unstated between us gave new meaning to the idea of seeing something through to the end. It was to be my subsequent misfortune that I would never manage to communicate to any of the parties involved that none of my preferences had changed. If all my former pleasures were affected, it is because from that day onwards I couldn't help but take my sexual bearings from him. But if they radiated out from his centre, it didn't follow that their orbit would be any less wide. And, as we were all to discover, it wasn't obvious – not to me or to anyone else – whether I wanted to hand myself over to him completely or flee.

From this day on, a man's and a woman's body, the delight they gave me, would set off on endlessly separating lines. But although they were never to meet, I could never enjoy one without it provoking my need for the other. To this day I do not fully understand why my desire to take things further became so intense. I would go in pursuit of him with a grim but enchanted sense of prophecy. Dreadful as it was, that first evening seemed to hold the secret to something else. He had made me believe he was the one who, for better or worse, would teach me what it felt like to be out of this world.

As a young girl, I had responded to my aunt's distance by going in search of warmth. I always felt that there was something about me that would never be coaxed into existence without a very special devotion. I needed the most scrupulous attention, alert to every fold of my being, from a body not dissimilar to mine. First I needed to be seen. My aunt scrutinised and appraised me and never stopped watching me, but I learnt early on that she was not really looking. I knew that there must be a way of seeing someone which is quite the opposite of having them in your sights. It should be without motive – a far cry from her shrewdly calculating stare. And because it wouldn't be looking me over, because it would be a response to having already seen me, so too it couldn't possibly stop there. Almost before beginning, it would start to slide into the next stage. My first moments of sexual excitement crept up on me very young. My passion, I thought, would be the perfect way – through another body, to whom I would of course be returning the favour – of giving me back to myself.

Sex conceived of like this is a peculiar art. I had been introduced to its pleasures when I was thirteen. My first companion, Lise, taught me everything. Smooth to the surface, anything but once she let you in. Her sleek blonde hair swept down her cheek on one side and was coiled behind her ear on the other so that, depending on where you were, she either looked careless or intent. She had shoulders which jutted out slightly too far – nothing else at an angle – beneath her slim neck and round, soft-featured, mellow and purposive face. Her eyes were bright blue, perhaps a little lighter than mine. When she lowered her lids, pale long lashes closed on to her cheeks like rivulets of water streaming over glass. She nearly always managed to look languid, as if stretching after a long sleep. A rag doll, were she not so devoted to her purpose. As I once ventured to tell him, without going into details, she was all but a mother to me. Not, on reflection, the wisest thing I ever said. She must have been at least seventeen.

Lise was not secretive, but she trailed her past behind her like a precious dog which, once attached to the sleeve of its mistress, can – as she promenades along the boulevards – be safely ignored. My aunt liked to send me out on errands at the weekend and I had passed her several times on the street. I would hang around by the baker's shop, clutching my parcels as though they were bags of sweets, while hoping she would notice from the way that I loitered how very grown up I had become. Then one day – like an older sister guiding a child across the road away from a danger only she has seen – she caught hold of my hand, let herself through the side door of a furniture shop, where she lived with her parents, led me upstairs to her room and locked the door.

Magisterial in her craft, Lise managed when she was with me never to seem exactly what we might call 'in the know'. She opened up my body, fondled me with talent, but although it was her hands, her mouth, her tongue that raised me to such pleasure, she always knew when and how to bow out, as if she was always preparing to make herself dispensable. My climax was her cue. She would draw back quietly like a fairy godmother sending me off to the ball. Never did it seem that she was displaying her art, or even – and this is perhaps the strangest thing of all – drawing on experiences which, because they came from a place beyond me, could so easily have left me feeling out in the cold. Not once did I experience her skill as a threat. It was never as though another history, other times, other places, were being proclaimed. During the time of our pleasure, it was all for me, succeeding in a way I now see as nothing short of miraculous in wiping out any traces of its own past. This was sex without memory and I would never lose the taste of it. But I realise today that it was only possible because she created a world which, for the shortest of whiles, allowed me to drown my pre-occupations and her to leave her previous sexual lives behind.

Because she was older than me, she was, however, very good at giving me advice. 'Don't allow anyone ever to think that you belong to them or them to you. It ruins everything.' 'Always move on and past, never treat pleasure as something you should hold on to. You will immediately stop it short if you do.' It wasn't of course quite as knowing as this, but these phrases, some of which she did speak with wonderfully uncoercive authority, give the gist. She was issuing a warning, but I was never to discover whether it was because she had lived a life according to her dictates, or the reverse. How could I? Her greatest gift was to shear away suffering – mine and, for all I might know, her own.

He would never understand the nature of this pleasure. In fact I think if he had been able to do so, he might have been more envious, more excluded – since its point was to be so utterly exclusive – but I like to think far less horrified. He might even have been able to imagine that, possessed as I and my women lovers always were of each other, it was on condition of a promise: that this would not be the finale for anyone, that there would always be someone else and something more. He might have been able to see, that is, that there is a way of living sexually which rounds on itself so as to allow you, in time, to stretch or pull yourself into another shape. If that hadn't been true, there would never have been room for him. His tragedy was that he failed to grasp that it was only my former and continuing delights with women which, even though I had to leave him to claim them, ever gave him the slightest chance of getting in.

Nor was this helped by the fact that he knew something of Lise's other life. When he wasn't courting the highest society, he too liked to make his way through the lowlier districts, sloping like a rat through the streets. A long time ago, several years before he met me, Lise had crossed his path. So he knew that she was capable of quite different types of appetite, almost the opposite of – indeed perhaps they allowed her – what she had so generously bestowed on me. There was another lover whose name I was never told. Gradually she brought her into our orbit. This woman was as tight in her body as Lise was loose. The moment she walked into the room, everything sharpened as if black zigzag lines had been scored across the air. She was, I am convinced – convinced too that this was the pull and the challenge – the only woman whose earnestness Lise would fail to subdue.

This was a woman who did not enjoy the same playful uncertainty that I did and so she found the world far less easy to baffle; partly because, unlike the two of us, she looked and felt far more like a boy, although even to suggest that this was the reason feels like falling under the aegis of opinion. She was rich and dripping silk, but her garments seemed a fraud. Not because, if you scraped them off, you would find a young man underneath. If anything it was her boyishness, too keen to be noticed, which felt untrue. Her lips were shut tight against their own fullness, her hair was cut in one straight dark brown line to her chin, her high cheekbones seemed to be trying to force their way out against her almost translucent skin. Like me, as I came later to understand, she was bent on a kind of revenge. But, unlike me, its object was her true parent, a father who had smothered her with a love which she had experienced as too much of an injunction to virtue not to be disobeyed. 'Dreadful, aren't they,' she ventured in a rare, perhaps our only, coversation, sure she had secured an ally, 'when they want what's best.' For her to enjoy a woman was, as much as for me, at least partly a way of defying what people expected of her. But the defiance got the better of her. It sent her after pain. Whereas, because my aunt had never really reached me, I could use my sexual life as a form of indifference. It was my way of disposing of her, of making her forgettable. And for a while at least it gave me such range that, whatever I indulged in, I never felt vicious. It was my chance to be − and not only to myself − genuinely loving and kind.

I still remember with appalling clarity the one occasion when the three of us took our pleasure together. By now I had known Lise for several years. Whenever I was at a loose end on a Sunday afternoon I would slip into her house, picturing myself as entering one of the salons whose doors I imagined always opened silently at his approach. I was by now used to her room, with its clematis flowers winding their way up and down the paper on her walls, a simple wood-framed bed with sweeping white curtains bunched at either end which we pulled loose to cover our little enclave, a candle on the tableside which always seemed burnt down to the same point, and the clock which − at almost exactly the same time every afternoon, a fact which both impressed and dismayed me − she would reach out to with her bare arm through the drapery to check that we were not overstaying our time.

But on this day all I could see at first was the glare − each mote of dust distinct, all the objects looking as if, sketched in too boldly, they had walked off leaving only their outlines behind. And then a scene etched vividly in my mind, yet also empty, the usual details of face and feature absconded, everything else wildly exaggerated, grimaces miming themselves silently and intensely under an arc of light with no source. As if my little band by the sea, which struck up at almost the same moment in my life – and whose fluency and ease was surely one of my answers to this moment – had suddenly pulled tight and hard on its invisible strings.

Lise was the artist; we followed her lead one after the other as she called us into line. She had the rarest gift of drawing me out of myself yet leaving me exactly where I felt I most wanted to be. Firm and precise, as always, but no force. Nothing about her ever made me feel I had been controlled. I was lulled by her familiar deftness, the ease with which she coaxed and brought me on before turning a more exacting attention to her friend.

She took a chance, gambling on my curiosity. She must have thought it would excite me to watch the pressures she exerted so discreetly on my body starting to strain. She must have thought I would be intrigued – although I don't believe she imagined I would ever be minded to follow – by the sight of a woman's face and body so passionately attended to and then stretched to see how much it could take. Expertly she prepared her friend's excitement and then waited until exactly the right moment to veer her on to another track. I could see the marks taking and fading across her skin. Although it had clearly been agreed between them, each time they repeated it her body received the impact like a shock. As the outsider, I was the only one who couldn't calculate her options, the only one incapable of raising or lowering the heat. It left me more exposed and vulnerable than anyone else. I had never thought I would want to be the one looking. I had never thought I would want to be spectator to the slightest pain. But, after the initial dismay, there was something eerily reassuring, even consoling, about it. Jointly they seemed to be instructing me. You do not have to be the victim of torture, either of the body or the mind. There is not much, once you choose freely to embrace it, that you cannot claim back for yourself. In my brief life to date, I had often felt myself the object of glances I experienced as withering, and the focus of an attention whose very carelessness made me reel. On the surface, what I had just witnessed was far harsher, although in fact each move was minutely rehearsed and impeccably tuned. For Lise, it was just another way of being generous. There was nothing, to oblige a lover, she wouldn't do.

—

Winter is my favourite time in Paris. In the crisp chill of the air, the buildings stand gaunt against the grey whiteness of the sky. All along the avenues the trees freeze into position, locked into the season and yet grander for being unable to move. I love the way the branches spread their detail, a template for the railings, balconies, trellises and iron grille gates all over the city, which seem embarrassed in the face of their rivals – as if once long ago they had set themselves to imitate such fineness and failed. When I traced their lines against the blankness, it felt like watching a piece of precious family porcelain yield to an invisible shock and then spread to the dismayed spectator its proud multitude of tiny cracks. I liked to watch the pedestrians hurry along the pavements, frantic to close the distance from one part of the city to the next. Muffed, hatted, furred, and yet so raw, so exposed to the discomfort which, despite all their best efforts, was the most visible thing on display. All through the autumn months you can see some of Paris's boldest walkers losing their grip on the city streets. My favourites are the gentlemen of the pavements, I assume on their way to the Bourse, every one of them dressed in the same thick black coat and bowler hat. Trying to look as if they are freezing for a group photograph instead of stiffening against the cold at their backs. It is the only time of year when you can see how heavily they are weighed upon by the grandeur, how oppressed by the magnificence of a city in which they normally take such pride. And the rattle of the carriages along the avenues declares to the whole world as much as to their suffering occupants how impotent they are against the pitiless force of the wind.

I waited till winter to visit him. I wanted to put as much difference of colour and tone between this encounter and the one before as I possibly, humanly, could. I was hoping that by surprising him we might together be able to skip a beat, come at each other shorn of the debris of that desperate and bungled embrace. I was hoping, even though somewhere I already knew how ridiculous it was to do so, that this time our bodies could be our cure. I thought a crueller season gave us a greater chance since there would be no ease and gaiety on parade. No larking about, no showing off. Nothing that could make us feel, if we didn't live up to expectation, not just frightened but such fools. At least, since everyone was more or less numbed and pinched, we would not have to experience any failing, if fail we did, as a reproach. And there was no sea here to cast us too far beyond the comfort of our walls. I was moved by his delicacy and by all that we had managed to convey in such straitened silence. I also felt sexually curious, suspecting that there might be many a trick which his too readily offered shortcomings were serving to hide. And at the back of my mind there was still the idea that something of more material advantage to me

37

might come of it all. But I also wanted, one way or another, to have done with him.

There is a world of difference between meeting in a hotel room and entering someone's home. At the hotel he had made himself a resident, whereas, in my brief nocturnal passage, I had at most been an occupant or guest. But we were levelled by the transience of the season which made migrants of us each and every one. If anything, my position at the resort seemed to me preferable. Since I had asked for so little, I could take it or leave it when it was time to go. Whereas those like him who had been more generously favoured were, as is so often the case, at far more of a loss at the end. As the summer drew to its close, some inhabitants drifted away, while others hung on. When they finally and reluctantly departed, it looked as if they were being dispatched. Unceremoniously, as they say, since the whole point of the season being over is that all ritual and ceremony abruptly cease. I know that in his case it was because his body couldn't bear the slightest change of atmosphere. He was a parasite less of society's expectation than of his own punishing needs. But anyone who lingers runs the risk of feeling they've been duped. I always left early, usually through no choice of my own. So I never had the experience of meeting a past life – one which still felt mine by entitlement – as a ghost. It was one of many times when I felt at an advantage, protected almost by just how loosely and out on the periphery I belonged.

None of this, however, stopped me from feeling foolish or at best naïve whenever I went back over that summer night. Regardless of what I may have had in mind, I had made myself extraordinarily vulnerable by laying myself out as if for a feast. It is not the case that I wanted all the power – I wanted, as always, just some of it, or enough. But the way I had offered myself had drastically restricted my scope. Like some poor distressed maiden, I had left myself no recourse but to behave defensively, no option but panic when things spun not just out of my control but beyond what was manageable for us both. If I was determined that next time I was to be the one standing, it was not because I wanted to wrest the situation back into my own hands. Whatever it was I felt so drawn to was far more interesting and inscrutable. It was because I didn't want a purely staged weakness to leave me running for false cover. I didn't want the dream of womanhood which I held most in contempt to be the only place, should either of us falter, for me to hide.

It was a Sunday afternoon and the streets had an air of defiance. Only those bold, fit or foolish enough to brave the elements had ventured out. They looked strained but elated, proud to have diverted the cold into a field for leisure. Having seized their recreation against the weather, they conducted themselves with striking show. Just at moments the exertion and strain seeped through. On this occasion I was happy to put my disbelief behind me. I liked and needed their resoluteness because it chimed with and fostered my own. Like me, everybody had to be moving with a purpose.

The street was unfamiliar, not just because of its distinction, the class of his address. I had travelled widely through the nights of the city, sat in cafés by the Opéra, hovered with my female companions at the neck of the woods. But the *quartier* of the Madeleine with its wide, open avenues, its mix of *haute résidence* and banking, home to the doctors and financiers of Paris, was not one into which I had often or indeed, as far as I could recall, ever roamed. It wasn't exactly stuffy so much as strait-laced. In fact in the middle of the day, as I would discover, it was a hive. But at the close of business the homes of those who lived there would shut themselves back from the street as if offended by the earlier frenzy, like a *concierge* pestered by an unwelcome visitor and slamming the door in her face. Although the buildings were not especially imposing from the outside, I could feel the wealth concentrated behind the walls. Guarding their property too primly; making all strangers shabby and guilty. Most likely I went unnoticed. I also knew from past experience that my appearance had been finely enough cultivated to allow me easily to pass. But the overall effect of the mutely suggested grandeur was to make me feel like a stray cat.

As I walked along wondering how he lived, I was sure that his house would be dark. In all these buildings, as soon as you enter, the light which falls on the surface they present to the street is instantly blocked. Although this is the natural trick of the architecture, it always felt to me that it was conveying a message: to be truly exclusive you must keep something in reserve, force your visitor to struggle as she tries to get her bearings, offer nothing unveiled. Further back in the courtyard there is often a well of light as the building, stretching beyond the outer walls, receives the faintest of glimmers from the sky. But it seems like an afterthought. If, after making the first adjustment you then start towards the light, the discomfort of having to refocus so quickly tells you, without any need for enquiry, that you have stepped too far.

His building sat across the corner of two avenues. Wrought-iron balconies were slung around it like netting. On every floor the windows were tall and grand, except for the top, where they looked like square patches cut out of slate, housing the little boxes which lodge those domestics not allowed to live in the family home. I think it is meant to be some kind of compensation that, cramped as they may be, they have nonetheless been raised to the skies. Barely reaching the third of five storeys, the plane trees lining the pavements look as if they have climbed so far and then shrunk back into the ground. His room, set right on the turn of the avenue, appeared to be staring blankly into space. I picked it out immediately. As the falling light of late afternoon was being beckoned through every last window, his were the only shutters that were closed.

I knew already that one reason he so loved the light of the sea was because he could not always endure it, and that retreating to Paris, despite the clamour and dust, was his chance to let his eyes rest and his body repair. All he had to do was simply aggravate everything most artificial and stifling about city life. All he had to do was shut himself from the day. Long ago I had known someone whose pupils were so light, their azure so translucently blue, that he could never sleep. It took a doctor of genius to discover for him that, if he shaded his eyes in the daytime, they would no longer be so thirsty for the dark. It was the only time they could look out without pain. Gradually I came to understand his behaviour as having a similar rationale. Peculiar as it might seem, it was – like so much of what he did – the best of commentaries on the world that surrounded him. A world whose vision often seemed to be in inverse ratio to its glare. He would be right at the heart of it, but turn his back away. He was in many ways no less bedazzled than I was. But he had this skill even if it was dictated by his suffering. He made me realise that to illuminate the tiniest fragment, you often first have to close your eyes.

On the threshold of his apartment I was met by his housekeeper. My first impression was that she had stepped out of a play. Tall and stately, she moved with no visible disturbance to her body, which was adorned in a costume at once formal and tantalising, the customary uniform of the most privileged domestic, shiny black crêpe de Chine in gathered pleats, pulled in at her waist and throat, but with beads glinting and, all around the collar, a busy profusion of fine white lace. Her head was poised over her neck like a lily on a pool. Thick, generous brown hair was tied back in a chignon but not so tightly as to prevent it from waving down across one side of her forehead. She wore no cap.

There was something weary about her which she seemed to be trying to conceal. Without any idea of her responsibilities, I was sure that however onerous her practical tasks, they were not the cause of the strain. Nor did I believe for one moment that she was really severe. Not, that is, towards him. It was more as if she was fluffing up her plumage all the better to protect, not just her offspring, but her own softness underneath. Her face was full but pale, like a plate of oysters covered with gauze. Her lips, which looked sketched in instead of painted, were slim but not mean, rather set against the world – a world to which, given her position, she would, at least occasionally and however reluctantly, have to speak. I was not sure how to place her. Although hers was the authority of someone who unquestionably belonged, she seemed disconcerted, not just at my arrival, but at herself. She managed to convey that her position was an honour and a privilege, but that she had fallen from, or perhaps had once expected, higher things. My hesitation was clearly a source of satisfaction. Contrary to normal

42

protocol, being thrown was the passport to an initial, although very provisional, success.

Later I would discover that Adèle was not to be ruffled, not even in the future, when I knew – however much she pretended – that I had succeeded in putting her in a rage. Eventually I would decide that what most infuriated her was an odd symmetry between us, a misery which we shared. Of course neither of us was his equal and, like her, although for wholly different reasons, I too would come to view this house as my home. A housekeeper is a type of voluntary orphan who puts down her roots in a setting that will never fully be hers. Whereas I was an orphan determined to redeem her social state. From the first she saw me as an intruder who would try to use this precious household as a way of mimicking her history in reverse. 'He's at home. Retired for the afternoon. You may go through.' She spoke the words as if they were formulaic, almost over my head. Then she ushered me through his door. Very little had passed between us, but she had made it perfectly clear, as if holding out her arms against gathering clouds, that whatever she might end up doing in my service, she would not be tolerating me for my own sake.

It took me a few moments to adjust to the extra darkness of his room. Glints of light making their way through the shutters, under the partly drawn blinds, were filtered by fine net curtains before falling across his bed. I felt as if I was witnessing the end of a long struggle between him and the rays of the day, one whose outcome was uncertain because it had left both of them so reduced. As he lay there with the light breaking over his features, it was impossible to tell which of them had won. I was stunned by the warmth. Currents seemed to flow from invisible corners of the room and then aimlessly but ruthlessly fill the air. They gathered so thickly it was as though someone had gone around lavishing paint on empty space. I felt heavy but also comforted. It was almost too restful to be true. In the longer term the effect of this room would always be, not to lull, but to harden our resolve. But as I stood there on that first day, I thought it was perfect. He had not expected me. In fact it was many months since we had last met. I thought he looked oddly casual, but decided he was merely trying to hide his awkwardness at being discovered prone. It crossed my mind, but only for a moment, that there was something peculiar about the whole scene. After all, the positions in which we found ourselves were not the ones normally considered appropriate for a man and a woman on the verge of fulfilling their desire. Above all I felt elated. But I had no way of knowing whether it was because I was genuinely glad to be once again in his company or because I was already sure of – indeed unconsciously planning – my escape.

This time I was determined we would talk. I sat down beside his bed and started to tell him about everyone I knew whom I believed belonged to his world. I wanted to impress him with my connections and also to see, by way of experiment, what would happen to such people if I dropped them without mercy into such an apparently inhospitable space. I also wanted to give the previous innocent kindness with which I had talked about my girlfriends a slightly different edge. Not to be unkind, but so as to usher us all up the scale of knowledge. He had teased me for my slang, reciting – as if they were his favourite lines of poetry – phrases which I blush to think of today. They entranced him as much as they repelled.

'Wash your mouth out, Albertine,' as my aunt used to say. I knew I would have the desired effect only if I could rehearse all the codes perfectly while indicating how pointless I really considered them to be. Above all, I wanted him to think I had grown up – that I was becoming a woman who, without taking on the worst foibles of society, knew how to run her social and sexual pleasures along her tongue.

I decided to sacrifice Gisèle, the youngest and most eager of the bunch, her blonde curls nesting in perfect harmony around her collarbone. She was always rushing ahead in breathless, glowing anticipation, frantic to mimic what none of the older girls had even begun. She embarrassed us. Our fool if you like. Exposing us to ourselves. I would lift her clear above the crowd and drop her.

I stood to one side of his bed and, raising my head, addressed my remarks to the blue satin curtains trussed to either side of the nettings and blinds. I was not performing for his benefit, I was thinking aloud. At each pause, my words thinned into the dark centre of the room like whorls of smoke. I could see him perfectly out of the corner of my eye.

'Gisèle never really belonged, you understand. We humoured her but we all agreed that she was crude.'

He looked taken aback, as if I was engaged in the direst self-betrayal.

'It wasn't her class. We made a point of being tolerant. But there is all the world, you must agree, between causing a bit of a scene and making a complete spectacle of yourself.'

I could feel him rising as he pictured us at the hotel. I

watched as the image he plucked from the summer tore through my charade.

'Don't you think there is a line to be drawn? We loved to turn heads, of course. I sometimes wonder if we went too far. But as far as more personal matters were concerned, that was another affair. We set very different standards amongst ourselves. Gisèle was not discreet.'

Now he was tantalised, as if it was dawning on him that our very public misbehaviour might be a front for something quite else. So I decided to rein him in.

'Poor Gisèle. She wanted to shock and then go on shocking. People dismiss you or even stop noticing after a while. To my mind, it started to spoil the real pleasure. I'm embarrassed to think about it now. It has taken me this time to realise that, contrary to what is often said, being outrageous does not take well to display.'

And then, consigning to history a whole period of my life that was barely months away, 'Of course we were terribly young. Unless someone was watching, we couldn't really believe we had broken any rules. We wanted to cause a stir more than anything else.'

With the room full to bursting with promise, I sat down on his bed.

'I like to go more softly now. My uncle used to joke that, comparing the French and the Americans – and don't forget that he had travelled – in France nothing goes on in the street but everything happens in the bedroom, whereas in America, where there is no modesty to speak of, it is quite the reverse.'

Perhaps the greatest skill of conversation is to make inaudible the sounds beneath the skin. Talk like this was my way of staving off the fear which still lingered from the last encounter for us both. Contrary to what I had just suggested, if sex is the opposite of conversation it is not because one takes place inside and the other out of doors. The struggle between them is far more implacable than that. For as long as I kept on, I could run rings around my own dread. How verbally dexterous I thought I had become! And how excited he was in response. My talk had made me brazen. But however far we went – and I knew by this point that we would get much further – it would not make us intimate. We were wonderfully on course, he seized my arm and started to kiss me. This time, I was not going to allow him to stop.

I lay down beside him and let him slip his hands under my skirts. I knew it would be different, but I had no way of knowing how. He had let me into a secret. And although it had undoubtedly made for the thrill, it had left us both gasping for air. What options did it leave him? To retrieve himself he would have to be accomplished. He would have to be deft. His movements were far surer than I had expected. Quickly he made his way up my thighs. As he pushed me open, I thought I knew what would happen next, but although his progress was as steady as it was predictable, he was to surprise me yet. When he prised his way inside me with his fingers, I felt myself tense and then give. All at once I became conscious of his body rubbing against me on the outside. Rehearsing this scene mentally, I had prepared for the moment when I would carefully but with no inhibition remove my clothes. It was not our mutual haste which made my boldness superfluous. He was in no hurry; he was unswervingly poised and sure of himself.

But what seemed to be exciting him most was not my readiness, the ease with which I let him in. The more pressing and urgent he became towards me, the more marvellously extraneous I felt myself becoming to his need. I was to give myself wholly over, but he also wanted something – not violently but steadily – to resist. He wanted a coating to his pleasure. Of course my women friends had warned me that a man and a woman rarely keep time. But I was unprepared for such dedicated ruthlessness as this. However much he desired me, I was not his main aim. It was like arriving late at a party, rehearsing one's entrance, only to watch as the host rushes past you to greet an unexpected guest. Or like witnessing a gallant fall headlong into his own embrace. By the time he shuddered against me, I knew that my presence had become as irrelevant as it was indispensable. He had given me a premonition of our future. He would become my protector – and then my gaoler – as a way of preserving himself.

'You are sweet,' I whispered. 'I like your dark hair. I like your dark, dark eyes.' I flattered, I pampered, I fussed. I patted myself back into shape and then set about soothing him down. Let him have the luxury. A few moments' grace. I would be unruffled. No sign, not the faintest tinge, of disappointment would show on my face. I cajoled. I wound myself around him. I put my hand down the back of his shirt. Now I would please him. Now he would take notice. There had been many a chord wanting. Bit by bit, I returned to the beginning and played them all. Meticulously, I ran his enjoyment back into every bit of my body he had missed. By the time I had finished, he would feel that his delight had been my work. Later that evening I could still smell his taste on my breath. He may have thought me bold, a little more confident in the ways of the world. But abandoned? I don't think so. I took advantage of his surprise and pretended not to see the slight hint of alarm which flickered across his face. He had thought we had come to the end. As men do, I've been told. But I would not stop until I was sure that in future the merest contemplation of his pleasure would take on the colours of my skin.

'Don't you have to leave?' he asked. 'Not at all. I am delighted to stay.' I stood up and started to walk around the room, like an actress making her second entrance when all the rest of the players were preparing to take a bow. This time I wanted to absorb everything. All along one wall, a deep mahogany cabinet gave off the only lustre in the darkness. White pleated curtains lining the inside of the glass doors peered out at either end like a shroud. Down the centre of a brown velvet chaise longue, pointing nowhere, a run of gold and blue flowers wove itself into a huge peony at the top, so dull and faded it seemed to be spun out of pale thick dust. I ran my eyes over the faultless depth of the surfaces, my hands over the tapestries laid across the backs of the chairs. The opulence crouched back in the shade. Everything was layered – fabric upon fabric as if you could never be sure that any one covering would be enough. I felt like someone standing by useless while a mother slowly suffocates a child with garments merely intended – she insists against protest – to save him from the cold. I had once been given a Russian doll. You were meant to feel ever-increasing enjoyment as you opened one doll after another, each time discovering a more minute version of the original inside. But what had always struck me instead was the crush. To go on repeating the pattern, the design had to be crammed into a smaller and smaller space. What chance was there for the last doll? How could anyone so diminished survive? Was that how you kept things in the family? A world within a world. A ghastly smothered little cameo of yourself.

This was his retreat. It was an honour to have been ushered, however coldly, through the door. But how brittle the softness made him seem. All edges and angles. Like a spider, his movements were constricted by his own art. The more he elbowed out of his corner, the more thoroughly he boxed himself in.

Now, I thought, I was staking a claim. Although I had crossed the threshold – and crudely you could say he'd made a break for mine – it would be many months, and I would have to work very hard, before I could be said to have arrived. I had no time to waste. As long as I hadn't really looked about me, everything remained wondrously intact. There was no question but it was his. Once I started looking and, even more, touching, its aura started to slip. Sitting poised on the edge of chairs admiring riches was something I had become accustomed to. It was central to the rituals of my social world that every object within eyeline commanded – it did not solicit – the attention of the guests. I hadn't always found it easy to get the balance right. Too much interest was vulgar, not enough was rude. If the host or hostess picked out anything for your appreciation, you were of course expected to respond profusely. To my mind, it had always seemed a bit of a joke, a shadow game with everyone pretending to stand upright while bowing and scraping on all-fours.

I stood in front of the fireplace, staring at the glass dome levered into place over the brass clock. His body curled and shrank inside the polished curve of its reflection like a genie disappearing back into his jar. Although everything bore his stamp, it all felt rented out, as if an over-eager auctioneer had passed through, branding everything on sight before the owner, whether bankrupt or deceased, had been allowed to make his exit. Never before had I found myself faced with objects so proud. Each one proclaimed its indifference, like a stolen artwork so famous that it ruins the thief's profit. Since it cannot be brought into the open, he becomes the lonely connoisseur of his own crime. I had been awed. Now I started to feel a little triumphant. Just by being there, I was making inroads. Without turning round to look at him, I could feel his protest subside. We had been scrupulous in the use we had made of each other. I think we would be genuinely hard pushed to say who had invaded whom. And because that was a question neither one of us would be able to answer, we went on being curious. In every encounter something was always left unsure. Creeping up on our fascination with each other there was now a slow but ungrudging respect. Don't let anyone ever tell you otherwise – it's not the sex but what comes after that turns lovers into accomplices.

I made to go. But this time I wouldn't bide by the change of the seasons to see him. I was leaving nothing to chance. Something had happened which in my little inner book of etiquette meant that there could be no turning away. Whatever it was, I needed to regulate and pace it in order to feel safe. He would wrongly read me. He thought I was now demanding the so-called proper form of a relationship in order to turn the courtship and the consummation the right way round. Although you might conclude on the face of it that not one, but both, of these stages had been missed. My anxiety came from somewhere quite else. Like a child forlornly watching a grown-up set out for the day, I needed to know exactly when, how, at what time, he would be back. Even though ostensibly I was the one departing, he was the one with the talent for making himself scarce. One way and another in my life, scarcity was something of which I had had quite enough.

'When can I see you again?' 'I'll come and get you whenever I can'. 'No, you'll be seen and my aunt will get wind of it. Not that she'd mind, but I would. I would never hear the end of it. I can come here in the afternoons. If you're busy, tell your housekeeper to send me away.' Thus anxiously, but fronting my allure, I began my other life. Without telling a living soul, I started my daily visits to his home. It was not what I had thought I wanted. How was I meant to explain to my girlfriends – they would have thought I was mad – that it was because I was so unsatisfied that I went on craving, kept going back for more?

—

Every day I left his apartment at four. We stole for ourselves the lull of the afternoon, when the restaurants have emptied after lunch but none of the shops have reopened their doors. I wandered back along the streets to the accompaniment of winding blinds and rattling grilles, windows suddenly illuminated with light flicked on by unseen hands, Paris waking from its midday sleep.

I have always preferred the department stores to the expensive boutiques which line the arcades. There the shop assistants seem too close to the outside, tropical fish opening and shutting their mouths in what I always read as disbelief, as if they can see exactly how much money I have in my purse, staring out at me as hard as I stare in. On my way back from his apartment, I liked, as I often had before I knew him, to loiter in front of la Samaritaine. I could pretend that nothing had changed. Because it touches the river, it marks the turning point where I know

I have left his world behind. I cross over the Pont Neuf and go down the rue Dauphine before catching a tram to the thirteenth district, past the Gare d'Austerlitz and into the narrower streets which run behind the Place d'Italie, where I live.

Only a few steps away from the river, la Samaritaine sits facing the Seine, which offers its grand façade a vast, perfectly reflecting, sheet of glass. At certain times of the day the light hitting the windows makes their display of goods and gowns almost invisible. All the onlookers on the pavements can see is themselves, with the river moving slowly behind. Gazing into the black panes and watching my reflection bounce off the water, I feel as if I am plunging into the sea.

On this particular day I had decided to make a detour, cutting over the Pont de la Concorde before heading up the Boulevard Raspail to le Bon Marché, which had long been one of my haunts. Not as classy as other newer stores like le Printemps, perhaps, but what I love about it is the crush. In le Bon Marché everyone mingles – the bored, chintz-covered wife of the banker, metal boots clinking on the flagstones, spending his small change and more; the baron self-consciously flicking back his tailcoat as he retreats into the library for the afternoon; the boa-feathered mistress of the famous writer, who, as part of the deal between them, has lodged her in an apartment with a direct view on to ladies' fashions from the other side of the street. When you first walk in, a vast structure of steel and glass dazzles the eyes. A thousand chandeliers hang from every level, vast rectangular mirrors suspended from the landings double the space and brightness in all directions, as though you were at a theatre where the stage lights, turned on full, have been suddenly flooded into the audience. Then slowly you notice that everyone is moving, brushing and touching each other untroubled by any distinctions of wealth or class. Apparently in a terrible hurry, they hold on fast to their bags and purchases as if they might otherwise drop them or, putting them down for a second, walk off and leave them behind. Now I am standing in a grand station. Hemmed in by the crowd but with no one in attendance, I dream I am going backwards on one of my childhood journeys and tearing out of France.

You can spend all day at le Bon Marché, but I was happy with an hour or two at the tail end of the afternoon. As soon as I step on to the black and white paving, I feel a sense of grandeur. One of a million, elbowing the crowd and jostling, but not for attention, I pick up twill and damask and brocade, chintz and lace and lamé silk. Fabrics exciting because they are formless so that anyone is free to imagine them transformed into fantastical shapes. I always buy something. If only a piece of chenille or a run of frosted gold thread. Or once, for a cream satin dress I had tired of, a silk cashmere wrapper of American indigo.

It was a few weeks into our liaison. On this particular day I had wandered up and down an aisle on the ground floor stocked with ribbons, purses, and haircombs, little bits and pieces which I loved to drop over myself, pushing pieces of gem-studded tortoiseshell into my hair, showering myself with deep pinks and violets and greens. I was holding a white cambric fan with, on one side, a deep yellow lily and the other, a purple rose. Twirling it between my fingers, back and forth, in front of a mirror to see how it suited me. Slowly I became aware of another presence, with a stillness which stood out from the busying, indifferent, crowd. Reflected in the mirror before me and multiplying my image to infinity, one of the long rectangular mirrors suspended over the central gallery just caught the corner of my elbow and the backward sweep of my skirt. And then a dark shape, someone who – from the position of the shadow thrown from the far side of the gallery – had to be situated out of my immediate sight, but very close to me. I spun round in time to see a tall man in a grey serge suit and soft felt hat, which almost blended into the samples of curtains draped behind him to the floor. He moved sideways, instantly wiping his figure from the glass.

I put back the fan as one caught stealing. And then travelled through every aisle of every floor of the building, all round the central gallery, partly in panic, but partly to find him or at least, by stopping and loitering as one does of course at le Bon Marché, to test – from a rhythm that would exactly halt and keep pace with mine – if he was coming after me. I stepped out into the fading six o'clock evening light of the city and felt his steps echoing behind me on the pavement. But it was only when I got a perfect measure of his distance – too far for an approach but too close for coincidence – repeated several times over the course of the same week, that I was sure on whose behalf, issuing instructions from the comfort of the Boulevard Haussmann, he was following me.

As the days passed, I became accustomed to my companion of the shop floor. I trailed pieces of ribbon or silk stockings over counters, like any customer changing her mind, so he would familiarise himself with my intimate preferences and, for lack of anything more shocking to relate, take them back and dutifully report on them to the one we had both left behind. Safe in his apartment, he thought I was his prey. Instead he had taught me that the best way to confound a pursuer is to offer yourself as decoy.

—

Strange as it may seem, in a way I didn't care that he was accusing me, vetting me, or setting someone on my trail. I always needed and thrived on his attention even when the focus was too intense. I nurtured his raving preoccupation with me. I wanted more of it not less. Whenever I sensed his interest might be fading, I would rub furiously on the glass to make it catch. Part of me wanted him to be able to see me all the time. So when I lied to him it was never simply because I didn't want him to know what I was up to. If only! – sweet dream that we could know and take on everything together, which I nearly gave in to more than once. Nor was it because I feared his anger if he found out. As long as he thought that was the problem, as long as we twisted and turned over my honesty, he was still possessed by the delusion that my other experiences were something which, even if only mentally and in agony, he could share. But there were no words to say it. Or if there were, I couldn't find them.

It was not – although you, he, would be forgiven for thinking so – because I practised to deceive. Even though I was to become an expert. I was never, that is, simply trying to cover my tracks. It was more my sense of having started on a life whose sundry parts would be incapable of understanding the first thing about each other. Nor was jealousy the thing which I most feared. It was the prospect of having to taint each of my discreet joys – and woes – by trying to communicate them to the other party. Hostile they were by definition, by dint of the thunderous noise dividing them, not because of a far more obvious, cruder, wish to keep me to themselves. To try and bridge that gap would not only be futile, but torment. The more he pleaded with me to be honest, the more I lied. By the end we both knew it – he knew that I knew that he knew that I was lying nearly all the time. 'Please stop lying, I already believe you.' Oh, he could be witty at his worst. But I still believe that I was the one most sickened by the whole thing.

It is something of a mystery to me now that I managed to invent a life of such perfect deception. From the day of my first visit to his apartment, there would not be a single person in whom I could fully confide. They were all convinced otherwise, of course. Have you ever tried to dissuade someone from the idea that you are talking about them to somebody else? Or that there is another person to whom you really tell the truth? I started to think that not sex, but talking, was the unforgivable offence. In fact no one knew the whole story. I had never been the confiding sort in any case. The intimacy I had sought from Lise had been not been of the conversational kind. But not needing to talk is one thing. Now there were matters of which I dared not breathe a word.

Worst of all, not one of them, not him nor any of my friends, had enough imagination to see why I wouldn't tell. In fairness, when I thought things over, 'I can't explain' would have sounded a little weak. Or calculated to enrage. As a formula, it hardly did justice to any part, let alone to the whole, of the affair. They all yearned to be Oenone to my Phèdre:

Oenone!
I allow you to see my shameful griefs too clearly.
In spite of myself my eyes fill, and I am overcome
With weeping.

57

I have never been given to weeping. And at no point throughout the whole saga did I ever, ever, feel ashamed.

But the upshot of their blindness was that, while I may have looked like a consummate schemer, I was adrift. No one understood that these small pockets of privacy, underwater bubbles struggling for the light, were never where I felt happy or safe. I may have revelled in and fought for my freedoms. But I was also frightened, far more than my accusers. I was the one who had to watch it, after all.

'Then die and take your monstrous secret with you.' My silence made me monstrous. Am I exaggerating? If I wouldn't talk, better, as far as they were concerned, for me to take my precious little secret to the grave.

———

Three weeks later my aunt discovered that I was seeing him. I have no idea how, since we never ventured out. Maybe she was just guessing, trying out her pet theory in the hope that it would stick. I thought she would be angry. When she told me, I flinched inwardly and prepared myself, as I had a hundred times before, for her wrath. I had just let myself in and slipped into the salon when I looked up to see her standing there, back to the fireplace, in a deep purple gown which seemed to swallow all the light and air in the room. Only her rings were glinting. Her arms were folded across her chest and her head was pulled slightly back from her neck. She obviously thought that the discomfort of this position gave her some kind of moral advantage. But then, after throwing her discovery at me with barely concealed triumph, she was all sweetness. I could see how hard it was for her to restrain herself. The novelty of the experience was almost too much. To have uncovered a secret which, just this once, was intended to work to the advantage of the person who had been found out. After all, we were meant to be on the same side.

'How perfectly delightful. How clever of you.' She stretched out her arms in what genuinely seemed to be my direction. We both promptly sat down at the shock.

'Well,' she said, with the haste of a gambler who places his winnings straight back on the table, 'what shall we do next?' She had barely paused to catch her breath. She picked up her satin purse and started fumbling inside it as if, with the right amount of coaxing, it could be relied on to deliver up a perfect plan. And then sat back beaming at me with an expression of the utmost pleasure and relief. She looked like someone who had found something she had been searching for all her life. I am sure she was trying not to weep. It is the only time she has ever made me feel anything remotely like a long-lost child. But just for a moment I found myself thinking – a thought which has never crossed my mind, neither before nor since – that mine might be a sordid affair. To her mind, we were at the first stage of a dream come true.

Now, she calculated, I was to redeem my past and all her efforts. Now we were getting somewhere. Either it didn't occur to her or she chose to ignore the question of what exactly, during these punctual afternoon rendezvous, we actually did. She would turn a blind eye to anything if she thought that it could advance us. And she could always fall back on his mother's presence, hovering somewhere in the background or threatening to arrive, in any case presumed to be resident in the house, as a way of bathing our deeds in innocence.

I had no choice but to let her become a kind of accomplice, although she could never be a friend. Of course, she thought she wanted what was best. She only had my interests at heart. I gave her enough, I thought.

'He is such a dear friend. He is far too ill to go out, of course, that's why he can't come here. But I am the one in his debt. You cannot imagine how much it is to my advantage.' I let that hover for a second before ploughing ahead. 'He reads to me. We play music. And talk. He has longed for such a companion, he tells me, for a very long time. I think I have become useful to him. No more. He needs me, I don't think he could quite do without me now. He needs me. Of that I am quite sure.'

I realised I had made him sound rather like an ageing countess lost for company, indeed rather like an ideal version of what, give or take the reading and music, she was hoping one day I would become for her. But if I responded to her enquiries with dull, routine evasiveness, it was only because I didn't want to shock her out of compliance. Another one rushing around with her eyes shut. Another occasion when it seemed crystal clear to me that talking would only make matters worse.

'What about his family? After all, they're so well connected. So well placed.' She offered this to me almost plaintively, bringing up her handkerchief to dab her brow and then, like an over-fussy nursemaid with a perfectly clean baby, both sides of her face. Would I please put her out of her misery and let her know whether this was cause for celebration or lament? I was grateful to her for being so blatant. It was like sitting in a room with someone who, for a reason quite out of their own reach, had decided to take off their wig. But I would have been betraying myself, far more than her, if I let her see I had grasped what was obvious to us both. We were staring at the only question in which, since the day I arrived on her doorstep, she had ever taken any interest.

I shot her a glance and then looked immediately away before answering, 'They only want him to be happy.' And then I added, as if the two quite contrary statements, instead of colliding, could somehow be made to add up: 'They only want what's best for him.'

It was enough. From then on she was unstoppable. I don't think I have ever seen her quite so excited. Bustling about madly, even though there was absolutely nothing for her to do. It made her frantic. And me almost laugh. She was the betrothed, all blushes and lowered eyes; or even the bride desperate to hide her fear of being ditched on the brink. She always prided herself on her social poise, but this tested her in the extreme. She had been fine as long as things stayed the same. But nothing throws a body quite like hope. Now she was fairly spitting in antici-pation. Bursting at the seams. For the briefest of moments – how could I refuse her? – I joined in the spirit. And then walked straight out the other side without her noticing a thing. Though it may have been at the back of my mind, the idea of marrying him, I should stress, was not at this stage my priority. It struck me as the least likely outcome of the whole affair. I have never been one to believe that the best way to beat a path to another person is through the marriage bed.

I had held back the night which, in the shade of his room, he and I had created, cloaking dark over dark, hush upon hush. I had withheld the essential, for my own sake as I thought. But it was not only my interests which I best served. I was not the only one I was protecting. I was also silently obeying the absent partner – for he was in his way no more faithful than I was – to our love affair. If ever I felt I was becoming giddy and starting to join in my aunt's dream, the image of his mother would call me back. One way and another, she was always there. I met her only once, when I was leaving in the early evening and brushed past her on the stairs. Her head was bowed, but I could feel her concentration. A faint, almost invisible, frown barely puckered the smoothness of her brow. For the briefest instant I took the full force of her composure. Our skirts rustling against each other, as we pulled them aside to let the other pass, made the only sound. Although we both knew from which apartment I had stepped, there was no need for it to be acknowledged between us. And the glare of the electric light, which the *concierge* switched on automatically when anyone entered at this time of the day, meant I could keep my eyes low. It was not that I was embarrassed, but that was not the way I wanted to greet her and she was clearly happy to concur. It would have made me feel furtive. I had often practised this crucial encounter and whenever I did so, I would look her straight in the eyes and be bold. Later when I tried to relive the moment, all I could recall was the mounted pile of her chignon, the fixity of her gaze pointed ahead of her on the stairwell, the steadiness with which she edged her heavy but stately body from step to step. Otherwise not a single detail, no jewellery about her person, nothing she was carrying, not one garment that she wore. It was the closest I would ever get.

How I had admired her from afar! She was known for her beauty and her grace, but I was most taken with her social decorum, although even that word gives her too much of a worldly taint. I had not seen her often, not even from a distance. Nobody did. Selective, she made her appearances more out of kindness than need. Scrupulously, moderately, but with total sureness, she moved, when occasion required it, through the salons and the drawing rooms. In that heady atmosphere, it was astounding that anyone could be so self-contained. She could take it or leave it, but you would have to be on the lookout to get the point. Nothing about her ever suggested the slightest disdain. Because she was so generous, the message she conveyed, if only with a glance, was how indispensable, unique and valued you were. I know I was one of several to have felt the afterglow of her appeal. In a way she made everybody an orphan. After all, I was not the only one on lease to myself. How many were going through the motions, making out they were happy – that all the insanity was perfectly normal – while secretly waiting all their lives for someone who would allow them to drop the pretence? You hardly had to meet her – if I am honest, I have never exactly met her – to feel devotedly in her debt.

So let me say now that of all the characters in this story, she was the one I became most desirous to please. It left me, at the very least, with a serious problem. She would never be so crude as to insist. But it had never, ever, been part of her ambition – far from it! – that I would be the one to capture the heart of, let alone marry, her son. Thus proudly and invisibly she took up her place at the heart of the battle between us. I would wreck my attachment to him, although I could hardly have foreseen how perfectly, for her sake.

Sometimes I would sit and think about her for hours. At the beginning, when I was so intent on knowing him, I was so sure that if I only concentrated enough, I would find my way in. But, try as I might, and even from what little I could glean, it was hard for me to see her as his mother. She appeared to be so comfortable with herself. A little fuller now, I was told by those who had known her for a long time. Although, unlike my aunt, she was one of those women who, when their bodies start to thicken, give the impression that something in the atmosphere is making way. Almost without themselves or anyone else noticing, they seem to be gliding and transporting themselves into newly available space. As if the walls of a room could round and soften by magic. There was nothing, nothing he could possibly confront her with, which she would be unable to accommodate.

Where could his frailty have come from? His father was a famous doctor and I know that medical families often breed invalids, just as schoolmasters often produce children who, as scholars, are inept. How better to frustrate your parents' expectations and make yourself the centre of their world? Even I could understand that it would be a fine way to reproach a parent for all the care he bestowed on the needy. And cruel, a wondrous form of revenge. I had heard the story of a doctor, renowned in our circle, who had stoically faced the worst illnesses throughout a long and successful career. He crumpled, his mind and body gave way completely, when he was faced without warning with the incurable illness of a grown and much-loved child. His skill made him impotent. It only made matters worse that he had so braved the world on everybody else's behalf up till then. He had the horror of a dying child and of his own collapsed resources to contend with.

If this was the silent arrangement, then her son took it like everything else to extremes. He didn't die on her, but he did the next best thing. As she filled and grew, he shrank and curled back on himself. As she made herself more generous and available, he dug in his heels and went further and further into retreat. The less he responded, the more she gave. Profusely, and not just to him. Maybe – she seemed to be hoping – those who blossomed under her attention might inspire him by example and draw him out of himself. But it was to no avail. He craved her like a drug whose benefits have started to turn. Like a sleeping potion which first comforts you and then drives you insane. Miraculous to begin with, until it becomes too familiar and you start waking up and counting the hours in furious anticipation of the moment when its effect will have gone. In the end, all she felt was her failure and his reproach. Her kindness took on the aura of her dread.

Did I see what he was doing? To her? If I had, would I have avoided what came next? I doubt it. But at least I might have recognised a little sooner that one of the things he wanted most from a woman was a very special type of clarity. He didn't just want to live dangerously, like any over-cosseted child as you might say. He also wanted the right to be angry. And because in the beginning there was no basis, because his life and her love had so cruelly denied him all contest, so in future that right would have to be contested over and over again. He would see to it. He would lay down the terms, establish the grounds, argue. Above all, he would argue. Even if it killed us. Whatever the cost, whatever the evidence, there had to be a sexual crime. Perhaps that was why, oddly and foolishly enough, I felt so safe. So at ease with deceit. Since, regardless of what I might be up to, it really didn't matter what I did. When he was in this frame of mind, he wanted me guilty or nothing.

PART TWO

MY NAME is Andrée Bouvet. I have known Albertine for a very very long time, longer than anyone I like to think, and better. Not that it is a competition, you understand, but I knew her long before he did, and after the end, as he became more and more desperate to uncover the truth, I went on feeling that I was the one, and no one else, who had been her truest friend, lover and confidante. And that I always would be. Perhaps it is strange that this should have been the result of his clamouring, but one way and another he always succeeded in bringing us together. Of course that's the last thing he would have wished.

It was my first day at school and the September air was balmy with the barest touch of autumn haze thinning the blue sky. She was standing in the forecourt and stayed looking up at the building after the rest of us had pressed through the doors. Nobody took any notice, but I caught sight of her when I turned on my heels. I couldn't make out why she was hesitating. She held her head on one side and was clutching her bag below her knees. She's terrified, I thought, although at second glance, she looked more like someone announcing, 'I do nothing, even when it might seem I have been pushed to it, except through choice.'

I could see she was pretty, but something about her seemed too big. The first thing I noticed was her magnificent thick black hair, which had been pulled back in ringlets, but tumbled out from under the edges of her hat. If it had been allowed to hang down loosely it would have been far better but, as it was, having failed to control it she looked somehow unkempt. Our uniform was mainly grey, tunics with white crimped shirts and panama hats, and shapeless in defiance of anything that might have been happening to our bodies underneath. But her neck was too solid. It rose grandly and awkwardly out of her shirt. Just look! A patch of nakedness that had escaped. This bit of our bodies – she seemed to be proclaiming on all of our behalfs – is there to remind you of what is bold, even if hidden, about the rest.

Her bright blue eyes were sharp and never still. All her other features were slight. That was what was so striking, such dark, dark hair and blue eyes together. I could feel my light brown hair and grey eyes soften in comparison and then go dull. But it wasn't just her colouring. How on earth did she manage to look so delicate and solid, fragile and resolute? I couldn't stop staring. Young as I was, I could tell that this was not quite how a girl was supposed to be. She held herself so straight and yet she was all frayed around the edges, as if she were threatening at any moment to slide into the rough. But she was not asking to be patronised. Nor would she. Not once in all the time I was to know her, not even when in greatest need.

As soon as she saw me watching, she started up the steps – towards me, if you're being literal minded, but it felt more like she was making a getaway. 'You can't catch me!

70

You can't catch me!' 'Hold on! Hold on! Hold on!' We
hadn't even begun. The air had gone cold and quiet.
Inside me I could hear a voice whispering, 'Not too fast.
Not too keen.' Then another voice mouthing silently,
shaping the first clouds of autumn on my breath, 'Can't
you see? I want to be your friend.'

After a while I would discover why she had stood there
like that on the first day. You cannot imagine what it was
like for most of us to be going to the *lycée*. We were the
first and we wore our initiation like a badge of promise,
even though we couldn't be altogether sure whether we
were pioneers or complete fools. 'Too much knowledge,'
my mother had muttered, 'for your own good.' For most
of us this was our first taste of life in an institution and we
could afford to be casual since, if we found it overbearing,
we could fall back on the solace and familiarity of our
homes. Even so, walking through that heavy school door
was an adventure. For Albertine it was different. She was
spending more time at home, if that is what to call it, than
ever before. She came to us from a convent, where she
had been for almost as long as she had known. An orphan.
Just saying the word made everybody flutter around
internally and stop.

However you looked at it, she was not getting a first
taste of the air. 'I felt I was walking backwards,' she told
me much later, 'through smoke. Of course everyone
expected me to be overjoyed, grateful even, but it felt
more like being sent home in disgrace.' And to a family
where she had never in any case belonged. She loathed it.
She had loved the convent, as those of us who became her
closest friends slowly came to understand, and why. It had
allowed her to be anonymous, to hide away, quietly
nursing her pride. It had spared her the ugly experience of

being reclaimed so loudly and falsely, as she felt, at the end of each and every day. You could almost feel her holding her breath as those final minutes ticked past. Down those steps she went, hair blazing behind her, always the quickest out into the rush of the city streets.

And the convent had given her her first love of women. That was one of the things she brought with her. Blood money. Her peace offering, her tribute, her way of settling any debts. Passion nurtured, and then licensed for ever after, because you are far from home. It would be a long time before I discovered just how much misery lay behind the carefully tended, fervent – and fervently controlled – attentions of Albertine.

It took more than a year for me to learn any of this. Albertine was not one to offer information, and our routine was so tight that there was very little time. There was always someone watching, although the building felt somehow dark because all the windows, arching to a point at the top – no doubt to elevate our spirits – seemed to drag the light up instead of down. Whatever the occasion, we would be herded into little groups, with any straggler rounded up so that none of us had the opportunity for being – let alone thinking – on her own. But togetherness was not what it was about. We were meant to uphold each other. With no touching and not much talking, every little bit of closeness had to be filched.

Pretending to have truly dreadful secrets became our best thrill. In lowered voices, with our legs neatly folded under the benches and two hands held apart on top of the tables safely out of our laps, we would tell each other stories, sliding them back and forth and adding little morsels along the line whenever we could. 'Did you know . . .?' 'Have you heard . . .?' Our teachers were our

72

favourite topic. After all, hadn't they been the ones to incite us by ordering us not to speak? I am sure that was why our tales acquired such a deadly and titillating edge. They were our devotions. Confession is a great teacher and we had been especially well trained. You spoke quietly to clear your soul of its sinfulness, and then whispered even more softly to fill it up again. We were the future artistes of the drawing room.

We liked to specialise in tragedy. Miss Blanc's parents had drowned mysteriously off a yacht. Miss Pouquet's mother was an actress and she was an illegitimate child. Miss Torrance had had a husband she would never admit to, who had completely ruined her by being profligate and a rake. Every one of them had entered the profession as the result of some disaster; every one of them had a terrible past. Why else would you want to spend your life cloistered in a school for girls?

All this made it much harder for Albertine but, when we eventually learned her story, it gave her an aura of mystery and power. She had lived the tales which we all lifted from the romances none of us was meant to have read, so now we had someone to give body and substance to our plots. She only ever spoke cautiously, but what she told us was enough for our imaginations to run wild. Her mother had died before she could remember. But was that true? On the scent of scandal, we closed in on her like hounds. Why did she end up in the not very salubrious home of her uncle and aunt? The diplomatic world she described to us hardly sounded comforting. I discovered, although not from her, that the Bontemps were once a solid bourgeois family, priding themselves on their sanctity and the narrowness of their views, with even an obscure connection to a baronetcy somewhere in the wings, who had ended up in service to the government because all their money had gone down twenty years ago in the Grand Union crash. And he was a bit shady, her uncle – after a brief pause at the Ministry of Public Works which he soon tired of, accepting post after post overseas. Of course they had glamour, but we were already wise enough to know that glamour without social acceptability isn't worth the price. Not if you're living it like Albertine. She had been taken in for sure, but that didn't mean that she'd arrived. In that family nobody did. Her sanctuary was a movable feast.

As we filled in the gaps in her story on her behalf, some of us began to feel uncomfortable. Of all the things she hated most, Albertine could not bear to feel she was being read. I would be the one to discover just how fiercely, but by then it would be too late. In time I realised that every move towards her felt like a potential insult, ramming her back, arms flailing, against the solid brick wall of her past. So getting to know her was the last, worst, thing to try if you wanted to bring her in close. Now she was getting the benefit of a treatment in which we had made ourselves expert, although up to that point we had been scrupulous in not turning our fire on to any of ourselves. Why on earth would we? These were not, nor ever would be, our own tales. Curiously it was our degradation not hers. Albertine always kept her dignity and her magic. Without necessarily meaning to, she was rubbing our faces in the seamy underside of our own dreams. I think she started to trust me because I was the only one who appeared to have noticed just how little she had really said.

Sitting in the class one day with her behind me, I felt her foot resting on the back of my chair as I bent over my book. It was *Esther* by Jean Racine and we were meant to

74

be learning it by heart. He had written it for a convent school intended for the daughters of nobility – three-quarters of noble descent through the father to be precise! But, aptly enough for Albertine's story, when the establishment which approached the great dramatist first opened, centuries ago, it had a hundred orphans in its charge. 'We would like a pious story,' the nuns had asked, or so the story goes, 'which can be sung.' Maybe they thought religious sentiment would go in more smoothly in canticles and rhymes. Racine had obliged, assuring them that every scene had been lifted from God's word, and that they should not trouble themselves about the presence of male characters, since in those days Persian and Jewish men wore robes. Whenever I read the play I wondered what had made them so confident that none of the girls would be inspired to follow Esther's example and start going after strange gods.

Esther had been a firm favourite ever since. I loved to think of those garments drifting around on the stage with all that carnage and treachery underneath. Our *lycée* did not go in for performance, but we were expected to recite the lines. It was not the first time that, unlike the rest of us, Albertine had nothing to learn. She took possession of that play as if it had been written for her and her alone. I remember thinking: Be careful, Albertine. Although I didn't really know anything about her, I was already anxious on her behalf that she might be about to reveal too much. There she stood, arms raised, her face looking as if it were sheathed in white, declaiming into space:

Death snatched from me the authors of my days.
But he seeing in me the daughter of his brother
Took the place, dear Elise, of father and mother.

75

From the sad state of the Jews, agitated night and day
He pulled me safe from the breast of my obscurity.

When we got to the scene when Esther risks everything
by revealing who she is and Assuerus reaches out to his
orphan Jewish bride, you could feel her muttering his
words, one small beat before him, under her breath, 'What
clime enclosed such a rare treasure? From what virtuous
breast have you received thy birth? And what hand so wise
reared your infancy?' Hardly, I used to think. But as I go
back over the scene now, she was surely telling us all
something. However much of herself she would give,
whatever pleasures she would teach us, in the end she
would go looking for a man, an Assuerus, of her own. Not
for his body, or so I like to believe, and not even for his
noble blood, but because only such a victory would allow
her to feel that she had first won, and could then dispense
with, the love of a world which had betrayed her.

'*Lasse de vains honneurs et me cherchant moi-même.*'
'Weary of false honours, searching for myself.' Albertine
did not exactly go in for martyrdom or indeed virtue in
any disguise, but as it turned out, she was the only one of
us who would be ready to lose the world to save her soul.

On that particular morning she had other things in
mind. At first her foot was barely touching my chair, then
it pressed a little harder and I could feel mine start to tilt.
Amazingly, no one spotted a thing. 'Sit up, girls. Don't
swing on your chairs. Keep your backs straight.' Then I
felt something gently pointed – it must have been a pencil
– start to make its way, so lightly that I could only just
register the pressure, up and down my spine. Almost as
suddenly as it had started, it stopped. The whole thing had
been a matter of seconds and happened so quickly that I

76

had barely had time to react, but I felt comforted. Not just singled out, but summoned, and as if every inch of my body had been stroked.

Out of the blue, I decided one day to invite her back to my home. She had made the opening, now it was my turn to let her in, first a little bit, and then a little bit more. I honestly couldn't say whether I wanted to talk, to touch, or to save her. By then I knew enough about her past to be sure that my family, solidly entrenched in the middle ranks of Paris's financial aristocracy, came higher and safer in the social scheme of things, just as I was sure that my mother, confident from the moment I was born that my marriage was to be a grand one, would find my friendship with Albertine not quite to her taste. So much the better for that. Girls of my class were surrounded by a generation of women dizzy with the prospects they envisaged for their daughters, while expecting to be treated as dutifully as if they were cold sober on a train. At moments it felt like a conspiracy of the dying demanding that we act as though the end were not nigh, all the while expecting us to join in the saintly hush.

My mother genuinely did not know which way to jump. She had only enrolled me at the *lycée* in the first place with the greatest reluctance. 'You'll be mixing with all the wrong sort. The daughters of functionaries, Protestants and Jews.' One of the things I loved most about her was that she was always happy to blaze her best prejudices across her chest. 'Godless and fearless. And no dowries to boot.' My dowry was the jewel in her crown. She had been saving for it with utter devotion all my life, but if for her it was the one safe haven from the perils of an uncertain world, to me it looked more like a slow steady drip into a lung inflating to the point of collapse.

77

My father was a banker who had worked his way up to the top of the ladder, where of course, above him and strictly unbudgeable, there were Jews enough. You didn't have to like them, and our money was meant to take us way out of their reach. Rumour had it that Albertine's uncle had been on the side of Dreyfus so one of my mother's objectives on her behalf became, I am sure, to wipe away the stain. At last, the right dose of scandal to allow her, with the grace of the society she had not quite yet entered, to pull someone less fortunate clear from the wreck.

In our world people almost believed that money could buy you blue blood. Was that why she protested so much about the *lycée*? Every family who sent their daughter was trying to spring themselves up and out, so all the parents were as suspicious of each other, and each other's daughters, as they were keen. We were all, give or take a few crucial exceptions such as Albertine, more or less of a kind. It took a while before my mother realised – it was her greatest disappointment – that the daughters of the nobility had stayed away in droves. As if the *lycées* had never been invented, they carried on as normal, trooping off to the better sort of convent, the last bastions of a dying breed. Or else, more often, they just stayed imbibing their mothers' best accomplishments in their homes. The irony! I am sure she felt guilty that, despite all her hesitations, she sent me nonetheless. After all, as many in the aristocracy would have it, she had shirked her role as a mother to the benefit of *voyous*, bunglers without a hint of class.

I will never forget the first day I brought Albertine home. We were both still in uniform, so there was nothing by way of social clues to be seen. My mother had to go through all the protocols of greeting – 'Come in, my dear. Do sit down. I have heard so much about you' – but from the way she scrutinised her, all the while pretending not to, you would think something dreadful would crawl out between them if she stopped. She seemed to be convinced that if she looked hard enough she would be the one to uncover the secret of Albertine's past, read off her social legacy and pop her safely inside her true class beyond reach of any further dispute. If Albertine measured up and survived this first blast of concentration to glide into an acceptable piece of our world, then my mother would adopt her – steal her more like – as a reward for her own remarkable gifts of perception.

Albertine had an impressive knack of staying obdurately silent while appearing to comply with every expected social grace. She relied on her beauty and gave nothing, but nothing, away. Modesty required that a girl should not push herself forward but allow herself, especially when entering a home for the first time, to be the recipient of attention and courtesies she would be expected only partly, and quietly, to return. Just enough to let you know she had received their message. As she sat there, back perfectly held, stiffly but not anxiously on the plush brocade of our drawing-room chairs, I had to marvel at the way she turned the appropriate reserve so perfectly to her own ends. Only when I leant back with relief on her behalf, did I accidentally glimpse her hands below the chair with her nails curled and digging hard into the fabric underneath. I didn't want to see, so I sat up rigid, miming her posture, as if to say, if I copy you, it will spare us both.

She sat there returning my mother's gaze and attention. Her eyes seemed to be detached from her body, as if she had briefly let them out to hire. 'I will fit in with you,' she obliged, 'but . . .', I could almost hear her saying to herself, 'you will never know me, however hard you try.' I started falling for her on the spot. Her face was turned to my mother, but I was the one who picked up the unspoken communication underneath: 'Now start trying. I will make it impossible but I will make you want to so much the more and nonetheless.' Unlike the first day at school, when I stared at her this time there was nowhere for her to run, except that now, with no less of an urge to hide, she seemed to be moving towards me instead of away. Somewhere between a flinch and a promise. Suddenly I understood that in all social gatherings in my world, someone – someone everybody feels licence to gawk at – is always being offered up as the sacrificial gift. But by now, I could see, Albertine had taught herself to court such dangers with relish.

Upstairs in my room, as soon as we were alone, I hugged her to me and held on to her fast. We fumbled and unlaced, pulling at aprons, collars, bodices until we were exuberantly undone. I don't think either of us had the faintest idea – not that day, not the first time – that our hands, simply co-operative, helpful, mildly hilarious at first – 'Come on, let me. No me' – would get more and more frantic, that, without either of us realising what was happening, we would be unable to stop. So someone else could do to me things which up till then I had performed all furtively on my own. And more. My little secrets. Nursed myself raw with only my best thoughts for company. How could I not be grateful to her for ever? By the end of that day, all the guilt of my lonely past pleasures was gone.

My friendship with Albertine confirmed my mother's worst fears and all my best hopes. Oh, she admired her all right. It would have been very hard not to, since she was exceptionally pretty, gifted and sharp. As Albertine got older and started to blossom, I only loved her the more. She was never a rival to me – we were far too close – but my poor mother really couldn't stand it whenever Albertine seemed to be sought after in preference to me. Now this is where my real story begins, when the world started to conspire. I am not calculating by nature, but even I could see – I would have been truly blind not to – that this unlikely development could serve my turn. Albertine had become an asset. How easily she had slipped from her role as pariah to pure gold. At least now, in my mother's mind, she could be useful. Whenever she threatened to outreach us, she could be reined back, with all her new worldly acquirements dangling, quizzed and plucked. She would teach us about the more glamorous, less easily accessed, outposts of our world, without our even having to look interested. From this point on, to my utmost delight, no one was more welcome in my home.

Even today, it still amazes me how often people seemed to go out of their way to unite us. How naïve they were! They genuinely believed it was their own interests, and theirs alone, which they served, while we simply stood by, quietly guarding our prospects, as they laid on occasion after occasion for us to fulfil our hearts' and our bodies' desire. Nobody noticed. Nobody minded. Not to begin with, at least. At the time, of course, we were elated, but now the thought of their blindness – or was it indifference? – makes me quake because it gave me so much power, even though I couldn't see it at the time and I swear I didn't want it, and laid her so wide open. Above all, and never more than at the moment when it was the last thing she needed, it taught us to revel in not being seen.

Perhaps nothing about my story is stranger, or more frightening, than this. Unlike him, I didn't want to possess her. I always knew she was one step apart. Who cares where exactly? What difference if in the great social scheme of things she was behind or ahead? But there was something else, a quality I could not get to even beyond all the social fuss, and no one ever could, which made me desperate, and then ecstatic when occasion required it, to be in the company of Albertine.

We were back at the sea. I had begun to long for a change in atmosphere, counting the minutes to when the season would shift and push open its doors. Although only my afternoons were his, it felt as if the light was draining from the whole of my days. Pouring into the tiny shafts and pools on his floor. At the sea it would all be different. Light and quick. Try me. Try anything. Run, run, run. Anything can happen here.

'Come, Albertine, my little cousin. Let me show you my world.' 'Let me escort you along the front, in and out of the hotel, into the society of the great and the grand.' We were as public here as we had been private in the city. It was his pretty ploy to usher me forth: testing the water perhaps? He loved our little masquerade, performing it wherever we might be, even more perfectly on the very few occasions when we were all alone and nothing in our situation required it. 'Come, little cousin . . .' Up and down the room he would go. And then sit me down on his bed and cover me with his kisses and his confusion, as if to apologise. He wanted me, he wanted to hide me, he wanted like any young man – he was not like any young man – to show me off. But even more than any of this, I sincerely believe his real preference would have been not to want me at all. To run us back to the beginning and bury it all in the sand. What had we let ourselves in for? Let's pretend it hasn't happened. Let's play at brothers and sisters, or the next best thing. Two little children at the end of the garden took off their clothes to play. What have we here? 'Come, little cousin.' His dismay spread to all corners of the room. I would have done anything to hide him from his shame.

Sometimes we would stare out of the window into the light. The wide sweep of his hands. All this can be yours. For the sake of argument. He was nothing if not expansive. Now let's see if we can share it. Now what will you do? I remembered one of my most excruciating moments as a child. It was a scene I had to perform in a play with one of my little friends – two girls staring through the window of a grand house, exclaiming with delight and envy as they pointed at the beautiful toys on the Christmas tree, neither of us with the faintest idea that we were never looking at the same spot. 'Look!' 'How lovely!' 'Look, oh, look!' The audience fell about. Imagine how much greater their amusement if there had been nothing there at all. But there we were. Peering out blindly. 'Their eyes met,' isn't that what they say? Two children eagerly straining beyond the range of sight.

Whatever the time, whatever the colours, the light always hurt him. It could be golden or, even more cruelly, a dull, thudding grey. He would narrow his eyes to protect them and then seem to draw the whole world into his head through the tiny space. You would think that to get through such an orifice to its unlikely destination the world would have to shatter into blinding smithereens. I loved to run my eyes to the horizon, where the sky joined the sea, and then imagine what it would be like to slip through the gap. Out through a line marking nowhere. Then I would refocus, pull back to the shoreline, slowly pick out the boats in the distance, white sails bloated in the wind, and bit by bit, as I came back closer and closer, the yachts drifting in the harbour down below. From the second floor of the hotel, where we stood watching in the evening, you could see their detail, almost too distinct to be real, picked out by the rays of the setting sun. All the paraphernalia of glossy wood and gleaming poles. Bagpipes of the water. To me their movement looked upwards as if at any moment they would float off making music into the sky.

This was where I wanted to be. Apart from anything else, it is the one place where I have ever been able to envisage myself happily as a hostess. My yacht would be all decked out with old silver and fine English furniture – we agreed it would have to be English. Quietly classy, a cut above the rest. But I wouldn't stop there. I would cram every inch of the space with more and more beautiful objects. Of course, the idea was absurd. No one in their right mind would trust their most cherished possessions to the tricks of the sea. But in my daydream that was the whole point. I wanted my legacy to be resplendent from the glow of the water. As glorious and fraudulent as you could get. One nudge from the elements, and the whole thing would start to tip. I liked to picture myself in the most exquisite gowns, admiring glances upon me, as they trailed after me across the deck. Then slowly, without my guests noticing, we would start to pick up speed. I have always yearned for finery. Dresses hanging on their folds to infinity were a crucial accoutrement of my dreams. But there is nothing, nothing in the whole world, which I have ever ever wanted to own more passionately than a yacht.

Our little bribe. To free me for ever. He thought it would haul me in.

'Of course. Whenever you want.' The deadly confidence of wealth.

'Are you sure? Don't be silly. I didn't really mean it. What on earth would I want with a yacht?' I covered my neck with my hands as the blood started rising up my throat.

'I will see to it.' He paused. 'But you will love me – you must be kind to me – in the meantime.'

———

As I think back on it today, I date the beginning of our disaster to one day that summer at the dance. I felt so sure, so confident, that all the different pieces of my life were safe. I should have been more suspicious. Mostly the fragments felt in danger of collision and I would put them at arm's reach, whereas on this day for some reason they seemed to be endlessly moving but each one gyrating perfectly in its own place. I think I believed that I could keep everything and everyone alive by nurturing my private knowledge. It was all locked away blindly inside my own head. For the first time for a very long time, there we were, all three of us – Andrée, he and I – somewhere in the same room.

In the hotel the grandest space of all was the ballroom. It was solid like an ocean liner but, since no one ever stopped there, provisional like the sea. Whichever way you looked, it was declaring its mastery of space. This is harmony, this is proportion. Magnificence which will never perish because each line and detail offers to every other such unhesitant, unwavering support. Everything in the room always seemed to me to be smiling at everything else. Wall to wall of wooden floors polished so hard that you looked down at faces plunged beneath a lake. Mirrors to the ceiling framed by pure white mouldings in the shape of ribbons and bows, so the whole room appeared to be moving under the skirts of an ivory satin ball dress. And the biggest, brightest chandelier I had ever seen, scattering its rays, bathing us all in glory, a chorus of tiny glistening gems raising their voices to the heights. As I danced I could feel its shadow hovering over me like a giant moth, wings in perpetual movement, while we slid and trod, bodies gliding across the floor, oblivious to its pale, barely discernible reflection breaking and closing beneath our feet.

On the dance floor we were all equal. There was so much light and space around us that, whatever happened, however distressing, you could be sure that something in the atmosphere would make it evaporate. Whisk it off. Or drown it – the waves would close over again, not a ripple to be seen. Without registering the slightest tremor. I am sure that it was the emptiness which made this room feel so welcoming to me. Vast enough and gracious enough to absorb any slight without a blush. We have seen it all. Everything nodded benignly in agreement. You will not be able to shock us. Nothing could ever go wrong here.

He would never dance with me. There he would sit, in his dark suit and buttoned black patent shoes, legs crossed, face supported in the palm of his hand, watching while he chatted to one of his friends. His thin black eyebrows, almost meeting in the centre, ran a stark line across the white of his brow. But he didn't look as if he were frowning, rather concentrated and haughty, if somewhat mystified by his own distaste. His cupped chin, as always, was slightly raised. His moustache, thicker now than when I first met him and curling up a fraction at the ends, concealed an upper lip with the fullness of a girl's. A perfect white orchid, pale but crisp, like an ivory carving of itself, was pinned to his lapel.

I marvelled at the way his eyes followed me round the room while engaging his companion with the perfect dose of intensity. Just enough for the other not to feel insulted or neglected. At least, if it crossed their minds for a moment, they never let it show. I couldn't even be sure that they had noticed the obsessive concentration he managed, throughout their dialogue, to bestow on me. For some reason, I was quite confident that I was not the object of their joint attention. Oh, I know that men love to boast, but they weren't, I assure you, talking about me. I could bear his eyes all over me, even in public, so long as it was strictly between us. Our affair. Wasn't that our arrangement? He was not going to share me with anyone. He would simply divide himself in half. With you I will be debonair. To you, a fox. I put my trust in his possessiveness. Wrongly as it turned out. His lids looked heavier and more drooping from a distance. He only ever looked to me like a dandy in this room.

On this particular high-season summer evening all three of us, plus several of my little band, were there together amid the grandest company of the hotel. It was unusually warm. None of us was used to the heat, which rarely crept this far up the coast. I could feel the droplets gathering on my skin. It was as if a plague had hit the town and we were all waiting. On whose body would the dreaded signs first break? It made dancing an act of cruelty. Gingerly, gingerly, we all went. Back and forwards, back and forwards. Arms lilting and outstretched, hardly touching, tips of fingers to tips of fingers. Hands brushing the small of your back. No whirring around. Not even a hint. Today we all had a secret. We passed it round the ballroom from one to the other without anyone having to speak. I felt I was listening to the ever-repeating overture of a concerto which none of the musicians had intended to play.

Andrée was busy at her own game. Like – but then again quite unlike – his. She was flirting with a tall blond boy to whom she always granted just enough attention to keep him both on the ready and at bay. But she would look across at me whenever the chance arose. I could feel it even without looking back. Of course I would be lying if I didn't admit that being so intimately linked to him and to her without either of them suspecting gave me an exhilarating feeling of power. Not the kind of excitement which would lead me to drop my caution. Not in that room, not on that night. I am always careful. I have long known that if you want to maximise your pleasure, you should always start by being circumspect. Tonight all my instincts in that direction were buoyed by the general mood. Who was meant to know? Who was meant to see? Are you surprised that I started to get confused? That I made what I now see as my first serious mistake? I believed – wrongly – their ignorance would be my cover. How foolish to think that just because you are in the know, you won't be the one groping in the dark.

It all started when the two Jew girls wafted into the room. There they went, all free and easy – he called them slatterns – meandering up and down through the tables along the side, their white muslin slipping off their shoulders, like two beautiful silver snakes. Only one of them had dark hair. You could feel the thickness fit to pull on piled up against all the laws of gravity on her head. Her face was too long, but not wan. Not a flicker of pathos. Such a large, lush face was the backdrop for features more extravagant and handsome, I thought, than I had ever seen. They swelled and pushed, against all posturing, into everyone else's carefully nurtured poise. Next to her her sister looked dressed. She was giving far less away. Everything about her was curled under and folded inside. But you got glimpses. Her eyes swept up to the corners of her brow, where they seemed to be about to slide happily off the edge of her face. Because she was so much smaller, she had to reach up to the arm of her sister, who seemed to be half lifting, half dragging her along. It made the taller one look as if she had chosen to go out walking accompanied by her marionette.

These girls were notorious. Shameless in a way I would never have dared to be. They weren't trying to shock anyone. Not like my little band in our youth, as I liked to call it, stretching years behind me like gauze. They really didn't care what anybody thought. They existed on their own terms. I knew that, in this world, we were meant to look down on them. But from where I was standing to be so flagrant was luxury untold. They may have been outsiders, but to my mind they embodied the proud spirit of the ballroom more than anybody else. Nobody could touch them. They could be sure they would go on for ever simply because they already had. Back to the beginning, they trailed their strength, flying in the face of a world that hated them. Would this be what it meant to belong? Really belong? A clan. Why mock them for that? I would rather – a million times over – have been lost and lost and lost to the world, and then left to create my own with creatures like myself, than lost and, as the final insult, picked up as I had been, dusted over, found.

I looked round the room for Andrée. She could be my partner. We had danced together here many many times before without the faintest hint of scandal. There always seemed to be more girls and women than men in the ballroom. Or perhaps it was just that so many of the men held themselves back against the walls, moulding themselves into the pillars. Atlas holding up the universe. We are the loadbearers of this great hall. Immovable. Of course he was never like that, even if just by sitting there he took on some of the stubborn superciliousness of their line. But as I scanned the room to all its corners, he looked diminished. He faded back into the glow of the white. Perhaps I thought that, because he seemed almost invisible, he could no longer see me?

I wanted to find Andrée because I was starting to panic. Those girls. I could see they had spotted me. Were they watching? Could we, just by a glance, eyes barely brushing, all tell what we liked? It is one of the strangest things about love between women – between men perhaps, for all I know – that it leaves you, in the early stages at least and as the necessary prelude to plunging beyond them, so utterly dependent on a world of codes and signs. If I took Andrée on to the dance floor, we could swirl around as we always did until they took notice. While pretending not to see. Why didn't I think of the risk? Why didn't I reckon with the possibility that everything would turn the other way round? I would use Andrée to send my silent message invisibly to them across the room. Why did it never occur to me that their greatest delight – their generosity – would lie in their frankness, that they would respond, metaphorically speaking at least, with open arms? They were so splendidly unabashed. In their eyes precautions were a joke. One, two, three, they started to sidle across to us on the floor. Mimicking us, showing they had got the message, and then leading us on, and then on and on. We were two duos on the way to being a quadrille. As I held Andrée to me a little too close for the weather, their wonderfully outspoken gestures started to work their magic. Let's face it, we were pushing our luck. Cheek to cheek, breast to breast. A touch such as no man on earth will ever enjoy. All the pressure above the waist, and a slow slow moistness collecting between our legs with nothing – girls can be confident, it is our little privilege – to show. But something had broken. When I glanced in his direction, I could see another man in his group, a real killjoy and spoilsport whom we had crossed in the hotel more than once, turn and point, flushed and angry, across the room. The effect was instantaneous. His audacity – his crude, plump, thrusting finger making tracks through the dance floor – swept the cover from ours. Before I had time to register, all my care, the whole beautifully constructed edifice which had hidden me to date, started crumbling. By the time we had finished dancing, it lay there in shards beneath me, vanishing into nowhere at my feet.

The divine Mlle Léa, actress and courtesan, liked to go in for disguise. Albertine and I first met her on a day when, instead of going straight home from school, we took off into the woods to play, after our fashion. I had told my mother, she had told her aunt, that we were spending the afternoon at each other's homes. My mother raised an eyebrow, not because she suspected anything untoward, but because she knew just how reluctant a visitor I was. I couldn't stand the house, nor any of the outside and inside ceremony and trappings of the life of Albertine. In Albertine's home everything had too much sheen. The reflection of her aunt appeared to bounce off all the furniture so I always had the impression that whatever she was wearing – purple brocade or green chintz – the room had changed its colours to match her dress.

It was one of those late summer days in Paris when the wind is so strong that you think the leaves on the trees will be torn away, when the brutishness of the weather seems set to bring down the season before its time. We walked along the pavement clutching each other's hands and our hats. We were old enough – just – to go unescorted, but only if we could muster a gravity harder and harder to sustain under the combined assault of glare and bluster. As the wind raged, changing direction with every minute, the leaves appeared to be chasing themselves in the sky, but the oddest, overpowering effect was to wipe out the spaces, the little points of light, between each one. We walked along under a swirl of constantly mobile but unbroken green which turned the sky into a glorious, vaulting baize canopy.

Against this backdrop Mlle Léa stood out a mile. She looked as if she had set out for a day at the races, but had pitched up in the woods instead by mistake. She always, as we were to discover, carried a slight aura of surprise, like someone who had been caught out in an indiscretion, or as though she were taken aback to discover she was really being watched. I am convinced she had an audience so endlessly attentive inside her own head that the presence of actual spectators somewhat floored and vexed her. She inclined her head to left and right but not, it seemed, towards the people in her path. If you looked very hard, as we did, you could faintly detect her smiling and muttering, bowing to the internal company and applauding herself.

As she drifted along swathed in white from head to toe, with only a tiny Chinese parasol for cover, stopping every other moment to smooth down her dress, she managed to give the impression at each turn, not so much of covering herself against the rudeness of the wind, as of lifting her petticoats, for all the world, to the air. We were glued. We were two girls, of course, but I imagine it was very hard for anyone watching not to have the distinct and thrilling sensation that they were being invited to put their hand right up her skirts.

If Mlle Léa found it hard to see anyone in front of her, she nonetheless had a marked preference, or so we'd been told, for young girls. By now Albertine would often consent to walk home with me from the *lycée* until our paths went their separate ways. She no longer hurtled out of the doors, although if I wanted more of her, which I always did, then drawing her attention to the theatre fliers on the Morris columns, the turreted towers with their bills and posters which punctuated the pavements of the city, was the only way I had discovered of getting her to slow down and stop. If you plastered your back against the columns, they were ideal for hiding, but you could also turn to face the other way and slither round with arms outstretched and hands spread, breathing in and waiting for the moment when you touched. We had often stared at Mlle Léa on the posters and marvelled at how her eyebrows arched, pointing up to her immaculate hairline and then all the way down the bridge of what seemed to us her unlikely, miraculous, finely pointed nose. Although she was only portrayed from the waist up, you could sense the promise below the canvas, how far in all directions she stretched. Oh, we could tell all right that she was a cut and thrust above the rest, and that she knew it. In most of the posters she was flounced and frilled, or she might have flowers in her hair, which to us looked less like adornment than outrageous interlopers threatening at any moment to slip down into her face. They didn't fool us. By the time we came upon the poster in which she was dressed as a man, with her mouth set, hair pulled back, hands clutching the top of a scabbard up close to her throat and metal gleaming at her waist, we had already decided she was ours.

On that first day we were convinced that she had seen us. There was no question but that she had paused as she passed. In fact, if I'm honest, there was no doubt in my mind that the one she had picked out, the one allowed for a fraction of a second to break into her reverie, was of course Albertine. I watched her waft on, massaging her composure back into place, but her eyes had moved to the side and loitered. She's going to leave them behind, I thought to myself. They seemed still to be hovering around long after the rest of her body had reassembled and then carried on its majestic glide. We were two girls with a crush in a crowd. Buzzing. At what point, do you think, you know – really know – that something which has grown and fluttered and festered inside you is about to walk out of your head? With as much excitement as Albertine, I could feel our little daydreams getting ready to break.

It would, in fact, be some time before Mlle Léa fulfilled her promise, and ours. In the meantime, we tracked her progress with devotion and on more than one occasion, we would have sworn to it, we caught sight of her strutting down the boulevards dressed as a man. It was not just that we had studied her too closely to be duped, it was also that she was clearly courting detection. Amongst other things, this was obviously one more way of drawing attention to herself. So if the costume was perfect – hat, bow tie, monocle, waistcoat, loosely fitting pinstripe suit – the gait was the thing. Not that she strutted, she was not pretending to be a man on the lookout for the boys. In fact she held herself with impeccable stiffness and disdain. Except that was the giveaway. The body held itself just a little too rigidly and then the eyes, as always with her, moved too fast. It was the contrast that jarred. We hardly, either of us – or so I mostly liked to think – knew any men, not really, except through their demeanour in the streets. On the other hand, we knew enough to recognise that, however much a man may be looking, when he pulls himself up to his full stature he brings the rest of the world, not up to the level of his eyes, but down beneath his feet.

By the time we really met her, Mlle Léa had already provided us with an entire education. Albertine, of course, needed no lessons about how to walk your own life on, and then right off, the stage, but she had taught us something even more important – that there is no better way to fool your world than by playing right in front of its eyes the very role that you are most determined to hide. Determined, or even frantic, as bit by bit Albertine would surely become, all the while sporting the wages of her fear like a trophy.

It was a Wednesday some years later – I remember vividly that it came smack in the middle of a week which, stretching out on either side, had been making us feel like a couple of idle, disconsolate drones. So we set off, as we did whenever the chance arose, to see Mlle Léa in one of her plays. She was performing at the Trocadéro, a place we especially loved because, while you could easily lose yourself inside its vast splendour, there was also something faintly ridiculous about the building, which looked a cross between a terraced city and a huge, white, iced wedding cake, crenellated and risen beyond belief, ready to snap and crumble at the first bite.

'Let's go back and see her. They say you can.'

'But we never have.'

'So let's do it today. Why not?'

Why not? Why not? It is to Albertine's eternal credit, as I see it, that I never found myself able to answer that question. Not even today, with hindsight. Not even when, as it turned out on more than one occasion, although not in fact on this one, that she was truly flirting with disaster.

Mlle Léa held court in her dressing room surrounded by what can only be fairly described as a bevy of young girls. At most there was a couple of years between them and us, but it was enough to give us that day the most delicious privilege, as one by one they stopped and turned and stared, and then cosseted, stroked and fussed. The steam and languor fairly heaved from the walls. From what I had read, it felt like walking into a Roman bath. Except that, since there was not a single boy in sight, everyone was the wrong sex and the half-naked bodies which met our eyes – since women are allowed to get away with so little – were technically speaking at least, dressed.

Putting out her hand, graciously but without a hint of ambiguity, Mlle Léa registered the slight tremor of mistrust on the part of Albertine. Then I watched as her body gave itself to the older woman, who drew her under like a butterfly which is urging its last strength towards a protector because it has been wounded, almost torn apart, on the wing. Not that there was the least trace of sentiment, pity or patronage in the confident and proficient gestures with which, before everyone's eyes, they then set about accomplishing their passion.

I have always known I was beautiful. And I have never been in any doubt whatever as to the power which this confers. From a time almost before I can remember, it was urged upon me by way of compensation that my beauty would be my passport, would raise me in their eyes up the social ladder, in mine would spring me from under their cover. 'So lovely.' 'There goes Albertine.' I could hear them sucking in their breath. 'So lovely. How sad.' There goes Albertine. Forlorn beauty, beauty breasting its own penury, beauty as its own excuse. Is that why it has allowed me to travel so far? Beauty such as mine, it seems, saves the world from envy. Because it never stops – or so everyone likes to think – apologising for itself.

I have always assumed – although how can I be sure? – that I take my looks from my mother. Everything at least about my face and body, which, as convention would have it, is pretty and delicate and flows. Everything which serves to fool and bring the world fast to its knees. A world not – I think finally – so taken by me, a world full less of my admirers than of self-enamoured connoisseurs buffing their nails at their own talents. I am not, I am sure, the only woman to have discovered that letting people comb her surface is the supreme way of putting them off her scent. Where the rest comes from, the bits that clash and swerve against my own discretion, I haven't the faintest idea. But I like to think that she, like me, carried inside her another shape, another life, and that – like me too – she struggled to stop that other life from being her ruin. Of course I would be a holy fool not to have picked up that somewhere along the line she must have failed. My true tale untold? Who knows? Who cares? No matter. I will defeat him. It will be my way, if not of saving her – after all, she might not need or want saving – then at least of beating my way through the crowd, past the whole dreadful lot of them, back to her door.

'What, exactly, were you up to?'

'Nothing. You're imagining things. You were confused by the heat and the haze.'

I bit my lip. I had gone too far, granted too much, since he hadn't said a word, yet, about what he had, or thought he had, seen. Desperate to undo the effect of my first error, I thought the only way to retrieve myself was to give him – by way of decoy – just a tiny little bit more.

'You know what it's like. What do you expect if you leave me to my own devices so much? It was you who told me about those two girls. I'm hardly the one to blame.'

I'd sunk them, but then, let's be honest, they were not exactly aloft to begin. So, I calculated swiftly, the very least I could do was wrest Andrée clear of the charge. 'We always dance like that. It would never, never, occur to us. Can't you see that you're the one who puts ideas into our heads?'

As I started to slip into a morass of my own making, I could hear his words, fragments of a judgement I had already conceded far far too much to, hurtling into my face. But they were all detached – 'brazen', 'odious', 'unspeakable' – with nobody to cling to, legless midges dancing in the air. I had blocked my ears – it would be my

98

only victory for now – just enough to spare myself the full measure of his barely faltering, stuttering but still composed, eloquence. Not one of his epithets would land. Or rather, for every word he managed to press into my skin, another one snapped off and took flight. The girls in the ballroom hovered around us for a moment and then breathed a sigh of relief. By the end of our struggle his words were floating damp and lifeless to the ground, as if piece by piece a child had been tearing the limbs off a fly.

It was over in seconds. Whenever we fought, it was only ever a matter of time before the tide would turn and the winds subside. We stood there, our anger dripping away or coiling back inside us, staring down at the damage at our feet. Now it was our turn. I walked towards him and put my hands on his shoulders, my fingers at first skirting and then making their way just the barest fraction inside the collar of his shirt. Firm but not too far. He moved his head this way and that inside the circle, tensing his muscles and letting them go. My body relaxed into his orbit. Jogging his memory. It was my only way of answering him. He could count on me. He was the one who knew me best.

The walls would not fall. Because we were no longer hemmed in by our anguish, the room started to return to its proper shape. But something had to be pushed away hard. As I lay back on the bed, arms and legs slowly stretching to all corners, I felt – not just that I was bringing him on and letting him back – but as if I was clearing the room. Doing all the work. Shoving against the debris of hate. Get out. Get out now. Leave us be. I could hear my voice whirring and shouting inside my head. Not to my other friends, you understand. They had long since made their exit. But to whatever had menaced a connection –

99

no, a life – which, the truth is, I surely needed and wanted just as much as he did. Anger, oddly enough, was the great healer between us. Right up until the very last moment, it bound us to each other more deftly than almost anything else. Drained us of all reserve. And then of course, with all I put on parade so as to hide and protect me, anger – flaring without wish or warning – was the one thing which always, but always, gave me away.

He felt the opening and wanted to touch me more, to touch more of me and more attentively than he ever had before. But I wouldn't – I couldn't – let him. Copycat. Now that, it seems to me, really would have been betrayal.

Sitting up a little later, 'There is someone,' he announced almost casually, 'I want you to meet.'

The fair Jewess, the one slighter than her sister, had lived with Mlle Léa on and off for a number of years. To Albertine and me she looked the innocent party, but how wrong we both were. By the time the evening was over we had all made discoveries, some of them exhilarating, some of them ghastly enough. I watched Albertine's panic run a thread across the ballroom to where he was sitting and realised that she was right in it and up to the hilt. I had known or guessed a little about their liaison – after all I'd been there at the outset and played my part – but not the extent of it, and in any case I couldn't, frankly, have cared less. I never saw her, in relation to me, as engaged in any kind of deceit. In fact I loved to think of her calculating away, provided it was somewhere – and with somebody – else. We had an unspoken agreement that, as regards her own future interests, she should and would always do, without any smack of inhibition, what was shrewdest, surest and best. Socially speaking at least, I have always wanted Albertine to be making waves.

To say I was frightened on her behalf would be an exaggeration. When we were younger, at the beginning, we had liked to toy with his menace, two children scaring a small bear, but that evening I registered something different, like a tiny, brightly coloured dot of ink on a piece of paper which, when you wet it, dilutes and starts to grow. Except that all the colours of Albertine's story would thicken and darken as they spread. So it would be more accurate to say that, although I wasn't particularly alarmed, I had picked up a piece of her own fear. Even without knowing that Esther – her name was Esther, they were Esther and Rachel Levy – even without knowing that Esther and Mlle Léa were so beholden to each other, I could feel the nets tighten around us where we stood. Perhaps too, unconsciously at least, I had some sense already of the sombre, terrifying, lengths to which he would go in order to get her out. To get her out, or was it to get himself in?

Esther – thank God! – wasn't having it. This was to be one of her finest moments, although by no means her last. She was not the bravest – Albertine was the bravest – but she was without doubt the most cunning of the bunch, as well as being the most generous, always at our service, as if she had learnt to put herself at the disposal of her worst fears all the better to pre-empt them. It made her observant to a fault. Sniffing out the present danger, she sparkled at the challenge, so you could tell that she had been here before. She fairly swung her sister round. Her pearl choker spun an arc behind her before landing, as if nothing would ever sway it again, slap upon her chest. Away from us she paced them, back in the opposite direction, step by step, inch by inch. With glittering poise and even more impeccable timing, she mirrored our seduction in reverse, undoing it for all the world to see. Anyone who'd swear they'd got the first act, would now surely be rubbing their eyes. Albertine and I just stood there, lost to any danger, overcome with admiration at her style. Although we hadn't yet made the connection to her famous lover, it was of course staring us in the face. She had turned a potential catastrophe into an encore.

Later that evening, when most of the company had gone, I sat with the two of them in the glass-roofed tearoom eating chocolate éclairs and apricot tarts out of hours. We ordered them from waiters who looked a little dazed. It was by now very late and we shouldn't really have been there, but we were on our own and past caring. Past caring, past everything, past bed. Celebrating a freedom as fresh as it was unreal. I suppose you could say we were showing off. Dizzy and sated with our own self-display, we chose our long-suffering waiters not a little unkindly to pick up the glut. We passed round the plates, glazed white porcelain with the finest, almost invisible, gold stripe around the edges and in the middle, three gold-etched leaves which by screwing up your eyes you could just about make out in relief. The cakes were all set delicately around the sides, the trick being to remove them one by one without letting a single crumb slide into the middle from the rim.

Without any warning, Esther lent forward, gathered several of them into one hand, made a heap in the middle of one of the plates and then started piling all the rest of them on top. The room went quiet and still. It wasn't just that the plate might not take it – an illusion, since they were of course each one as light as air. Nor that it made them look so indecorous, as if the chocolate might start melting into the fruit. It was something about her gesture, the way she hunched herself forward, muslin crumpled between her knees, and the intentness of the expression on her face. She gripped them just that little bit too tightly, like someone with a sore tooth who pokes out their tongue to hide the ache, or someone clutching their stomach after a knife has ripped through their back. Her sister's dark eyes fell on Esther's hands. She's used to this, I thought. It was clearly not the first time she had retired in her younger sister's favour, fading out quietly, making way for her to speak this clumsily but plainly on everyone else's behalf. We had been triumphant but we were also distraught. Nobody was playing any more. And then it dawned on us. Not one of us knew — in fact we had no idea — what had happened to Albertine.

In the early days, before it became too much for him, he would sometimes sit by the shore and watch the sons of the aristocracy ride along on horseback in the evening sun. Maybe he hoped to pick up, from the sand they kicked over him in passing, everything best, noblest and strongest about their pedigree. He would never admit it, but, however tenderly he nursed his own weakness, I am convinced he cherished a belief that one morning he would wake up and find his body, his breathing, his posture — all of it — in mint condition, miraculously renewed and repaired. How often did I see him adjusting his collar and his shirt in one mirror, with another carefully positioned behind him so he could inspect all angles, stiffen his limbs like a tin soldier and then nonchalantly, as if being casual were the true performance, release his body from the strain. Sometimes I think he loved mine with so violent a passion only because of the loathing he felt – not always, but just as intensely – for his own. Is that why things turned so ugly? Ugly does as ugly is. There he was, the little dwarf inside him, ranting and tearing his own hair.

It was one of these young men from the shore whom he wanted me to meet. Octave, who had at least taken the trouble to notice him, and one day had wheeled round his horse and gone back to ask him what he was doing sitting there so wretched on the sand. They had struck up a conversation, and from there a friendship, which relied a great deal on his discovering that this Octave was something of a fraud and a poseur. Far from being noble, he was the son of one of the richest industrial magnates in France. He sported his father's wealth with a brashness which you would think – I always had my sharpest eye out for such matters – would brand him unmistakably as *nouveau*. But something about his carelessness, his stunning good looks and permanently bronzed skin let him through. Or almost. As soon as we were introduced, I recognised Octave as the toff who could be made out almost daily in the bay gliding back and forwards from one of the more distant yachts on a skiff. He was all speed and swagger – a real swell, as they say – but even I could see that his sweeping and monotonously repeated circles were a way of showing that he really didn't know quite how or where to place himself. His blond hair was swept back and he had a permanent smile, teeth glinting as though someone had brushed them with white powder which had obligingly melted into a glossy white paste and then stuck. He was as uneasy as ease can get.

Octave had another side to him. Unusually in his case,

or rather for the world we moved in, his front really was a front. It acted as a cover, with proud monumental superficiality, for something far more interesting and sceptical, of which he was not a little ashamed. He was another one making forced landings. In the long run our friendship would be based on this. As indeed would theirs. After all, he was the one who had stopped his horse while the others had gone careering on their way oblivious to our diminutive spectator on the shore. At least he had managed to see himself being seen, without taking it as just one more brush of his own polish. And he had plucked my friend off the sands, a little contemptuously maybe to begin with, but also because he knew – without quite being able to do anything about it – that the more perfectly he staged himself in society, the less progress he made. He was getting nowhere in a big hurry.

Octave was used to being loved for his body. He never stopped displaying his assets. But it was obvious to me that he felt almost cursed by his – truly exceptional – prowess. I don't think he had ever met anyone before who was capable of admiring him, as my friend did so openly without ever letting his admiration wane, at the same time as offering him, with no apparent trace of resentment, such a caricatured replica of Octave's own self-disgust. Whenever he smiled his broad smile, his piercing blue eyes, a bit glazed, a bit too sharp, seemed to be making a quite different plea, 'This is ridiculous. For God's sake, help me to stop.' It was not of course what was meant to be going on between us. But I immediately found myself happy, far more than happy, to consent.

We sat sipping tea, staring out at the bay, each of us scouring it for ways out of our dilemma. It was like being at a masked ball where all the guests, without consulting each other, had chosen to sport a mildly exaggerated portrait of their own face. I was obviously meant to fall for Octave there and then. At the mere sight of all those muscles, I was meant to know exactly what to do next. As a way of restoring me to myself. And from there – although quite how the next stage was to work I wasn't sure – back to him. Tragically – if it were not so comic – I think he genuinely believed that contact with a man's body such as this one would do the trick. Could he imagine it? Did he like the idea? Was he really willing to go that far? Stripping us both naked in his mind as the only sure way of dressing down all my errors. Smoking them out. He must have thought – how wrong he was – that I turned to the women in my life because he was too feeble. That whatever we got up to together, my love for them served – as the cold cruel core of our pleasure – to make a mockery of him. 'Octave,' he broke the silence. In unison the two of them uncrossed and then recrossed their legs. 'My little cousin would love it if you would take her to visit an aerodrome.'

We headed out the next day. When he wasn't in his boat, Octave liked best to drive at speed. He dispatched his chauffeur and picked me up at the front of the jetty, where the road from the countryside started its long slow curve round to the hotel. If we'd set off less furtively, I'm still not sure that we would have been noticed, nor quite honestly whether it would have mattered if we had been. A kind of languor had set in on the season. More and more, people seemed to like it when someone broke the odd rule. As long as you didn't go too far, they were provided with the twin satisfaction of letting nothing escape them and of turning a blind eye. But we were pleased at our little bit of secrecy. It made the excursion, which I was of course determined to keep wholly innocent, feel slightly risqué. Even if nothing was about to occur, we were in something together. It was our opening sop to him.

Octave bent over the steering wheel with his chin jutting out over its frame. He looked extremely uncomfortable, but he clearly believed that this part of his vehicle should have the benefit of as much of his body as possible. A car needs coaxing, as they say. I wasn't quite sure where to look, since it felt as if I was overhearing a very intimate conversation which at any moment might turn into an ugly domestic scene. I couldn't tell whether the juddering of the motor was the prelude to something grander or whether our whole adventure was about to come to a premature stop. But Octave was dedicated, drawing out the levers, pressing and releasing his foot, tuning and pumping for all he was worth. When the motor started to pick up speed, he leant back, arms stretched in front of him, as distant now as he had been close up till then. Now he had taught his beloved vehicle all the skills and it was moving so smoothly to his purpose, he could let go.

I have never quite worked out what a woman is meant to do in a motorcar. I knew that, unlike Octave, our shared friend – as we now referred to him – loved to be driven around. And I had often marvelled at the way his body seemed to suspend its agonies for the ride. I think it was something to do with the fact that in no other situation could he so happily unite the joys of such luxurious safety – being looked after, carried along with no exertion – with the exhilaration of what was after all, at least potentially, a deadly stunt. If this was danger, he was not the guilty party. It was the only time I ever felt him breathing without effort. With so much pressure from the outside, how could his body, even had it wanted to thwart him, hope to compete? Just for a while, he was a conqueror defying his own weakness while sitting perfectly still. A man who could take – who could do – anything, provided there was in fact nothing whatsoever for him to do.

Not for me. I would sit in the passenger seat feeling superfluous and mildly insulted even though, I have to admit, there was something about it that I loved. Not exactly the speed, nothing to do with making headway, but what it did to my skin as the air rushed against my face. As the trees and fields raced backwards, it always seemed to me that they were gently mocking those accompanying me, my blither companions of the motor-car. Whatever they had in mind, I was going the other way. Clawed right back without protest to before the world began. After all, how do you know which bit is really moving? How can you tell, until the car stops at what is meant to be your destination, whether you have in fact gone anywhere at all? As a child I had always loved those booths at the fairground, where a paper picture of a landscape, painted in minute and garish detail, rotates the whole world along beside you as you sit. That is the kind of motion I like best. I don't want to be taken anywhere. I prefer to have the ground unmoving beneath my feet.

Octave kept his eyes steadily on the road and never looked at me once during the whole trip. But by the time we drew up outside the aerodrome, he knew he was in the dark. 'Here we are then,' he announced, not quite pompously, but with a confidence he didn't believe in, like a small boy on whom it is slowly dawning that, although he may have followed the manual to the letter, his gadget is about to fall apart. He clambered out of the car and came round the side to help me out with an impressive minimum of gallantry. It was the least he could do. I had barely touched the ground, before, in perfect harmony, we lifted our eyes gratefully up to the sky. The scapegoat for our embarrassment. Behind us we could hear the noise of mechanics towing one craft away from the landing base. We were just in time to see another one, more air than substance, straining itself against the wind. I didn't believe that it could possibly make it. We watched it rise, a fuming contraption of bits and pieces, all joints and rivets and metal shafts. Less flying than grinding its way into a sky which seemed to have all the density on its side, like someone starting an argument puffing themselves out with their own weight. A bicycle on its way to being a bird. By the time we realised we had lost the sound, it was hovering in a whorl of air, almost motionless, silently signalling victory to the watchers beneath.

It wasn't the freedom I loved most – I have never wanted to fly. After all, what exactly would I be free of, since I would still have myself for company? What excited me was the way the aeroplane shrank and shrank, glinting and then disappearing against the blue, for every succeeding effort losing itself more and more to the sky. The only creatures in the world who know, as they exert their monumental power, how to make themselves scarce. A power which knows how to float off, shedding itself as it goes. The kind that couldn't care less. Believe me, it is the only one in the world worth having.

Octave and a number of the onlookers broke into applause. He looked mildly triumphant. In the end, I suppose, it had been a victory or even a seduction of sorts. But when we groped together, after he suddenly stopped the car with no announcement on the way back, he seemed almost as surprised and discomfited as I was. There we sat going through the motions, in obedience perhaps to our absent maestro, for a good while after our bodies, let alone common sense, told us to stop. But we couldn't have been further from fulfilling his dictates. We were two clumsy, befuddled, overgrown children, excited by their own dread – furtive and on the lookout. Everything pulled back and dissolved. The sky beat down on empty space. With no one for miles around, we were terrified that at any moment we would be caught.

When I look back over those last months – it went on for almost a year and hasn't really stopped – the question I keep asking myself is whether she knew what she was doing. Or not. It is very hard for me, perhaps the hardest thing of all, to think that Albertine could ever have let anything spin beyond her control. She was so elegant of purpose. Ever since I'd first met her, she struck me as someone who was already, even as a girl, weaving her own web, turning herself into the accomplished crafts-woman of her fate. You couldn't back Albertine up against a wall to save your life.

PART THREE

INSIDE THIS house I have felt safe for the first time. To begin with at least, when we returned to the city, it was like being on a train, destination chosen, ticket purchased, sitting in my seat with nothing more to decide. This is not one of the trains of my childhood. I am on my own. What I love about these journeys is being taken somewhere by someone you never have to see, who knows absolutely nothing about why you are there. And if they have no clue as to your final destination when you leave them, even less can they envisage – for it is of absolutely no interest – what might, for the duration of a journey during which you rely on them so totally, be going on inside your mind. A little contract to which neither of the parties have signed. I will enclose you in this space, carry you in this cradle, even rock you to sleep, and then put you down, without protest or remark, where and when you choose. And the dreams you dream all the while are strictly none of my affair.

At the *lycée*, I remember asking one of our teachers what I could see was a real poser. Imagine an open carriage – however unlikely – with a passenger who suddenly, for the pure hell of it, jumps as high as she can, bringing up her knees, holding on fast in her own little bubble, so she loses just for a fraction of a second all contact with the train. When she finally landed, as land I realised she must, would she, I asked with deadly seriousness, return to the same spot? Or would the train sweep on underneath her while she was airborne, so that when her feet touched down on the carriage once more, she would find herself a little way further back? And when the teacher eventually answered, 'The same place', since she will move at the speed of the train, I was never, but never, convinced. I knew that there was no world so finely regulated that I could not leap free of it, if only for the barest instant. That instant was everything. Should the going get ugly, I was sure it was all I would need.

In the past few weeks I have often had recourse to that image of a little girl leaping – past the obduracy of teacher and train – up and down, up and down, in the air. Today, I notice that it isn't quite working. She was meant to be for me, for my pleasure alone, but now it looks more as if I am screaming for attention. Not stretching out, a body held in the perfect equilibrium of its aim, but not quite dangling either. Let your body go, they always told me, as you fall. Now what I see are limbs gone stiff, an overwound, speeded-up, clockwork toy.

When he said we were returning early to Paris, it did seem, I must say, a solution of sorts. 'Things will be different from now on. I want you to be with me the whole time. It is a way,' I was not persuaded by this, 'of normalising our affair.' And because he had so perfectly dosed me up till then, with only little drops of his medicine, I was by this stage craving to get my own hands on the bottle and pour the whole lot down my throat. So I agreed. But the condition for both of us, without it ever having to be stated, was that nothing would ever be said about what had happened – what *had* happened? – before. Thus cautiously we each circled round the other's position, like two insects testing out the ground for contact by first lifting and putting down their feelers on the same spot. We locked ourselves into a silence of our own choosing. For reasons so completely at odds that to talk of them would tear open not just our mundane arrangements but the very fabric of our souls. He thought silence was a giveaway. I thought it was a cloak. Now we know. But now, of course, it is too late.

My room is to one side of his, along a short corridor into the body of the apartment, the *petit salon* intended for receiving guests and for the minimal etiquette of dining. Since he does everything in his bedroom and never, as I have discovered, exactly dines, it had, from almost the time he took up residency here, fallen into disuse. And so it had remained long after it had been transformed into a guest room which had visibly – lovingly, laboriously, with the finest eye for every need and detail – been made up for a female occupant whose presence, stamped on every object before me, is all the more tangible for its being so transparent that she did not exist. Until I arrived? On such sweet and pained uncertainty we have been feeding too long. Beside the bed, on a small deep mahogany table draped with lace, sits a glass drinking cup, a half-empty bottle of Vichy water, a partly burned candle, and a bunch of *tilleul*, as if she has just stepped from a troubled sleep. At times, this room has felt like a mould, beautifully sculpted, perfectly shaped all around the sides – look what I can make! But no base, nothing behind or underneath, liquid pouring into a void. So much for my comings and goings.

115

They have, I think, made no difference at all. We have agonised, together and apart, over my every move and worn our spirits thin. All around this apartment I can see the traces of our desperate intent. These traces make their own way now, with no need of us any more. Bit by bit we have made ourselves disposable. At least, I tell myself, I can take solace in the fact that, although no one else has lived here, I am not the first person who has not inhabited this room. A room emptied of my presence before I arrived. So I can leave, as the saying goes, with a good grace.

Everything around me is golden and beige and blue. All up the walls, over silken paper, run thin and parallel lines of deep sapphire carving into the expanse of soft fawn and pushing it backwards, so it looks as if at any moment the whole surface might fall away. And from ceiling to floor between each set of stripes, there are rows of *fleurs-de-lis*, in the same crystal blue, lining up to do service to the gently controlled opulence. Over time these flowers have become very important to me. After all, stripes are meant to go marching – there is not a lot else they can do. But it takes far more, a far greater strain of artifice, to turn flowers so preternaturally blue and freeze them into such daunting and flawless precision.

Almost from head to toe, my bed is covered with gold satin. It looks like a fairy ball dress except that a little bit of wood has been allowed to emerge all along the top of the headrest, as if midway you have suddenly switched stories and moved to the one about the woodcutter honing his craft among the trees. When I lie down, arch my back and look up, wooden roses rise above me, the petals coiling deep into their dark. For some reason – I think it must have been a bad joke – pink ribbons are tied at intervals around the side. But the roses are mine. How many times

116

have I followed the folds of their segments, thick to scratch on, into and out of my own pain.

There is a beige satin footrest and a chair to match, with iron pins skirting round its back. A perfect circle of little studs pressed into the body of the fabric, holding it tight to the frame. The rest of the chair then swells and plumps itself, as if in response. In this room you never know what will strike the senses first. A world almost too soft to lie on, so cushioned you could fall right through it and out the other side. Or a world bearing the tiny scars of force, moments of a more violent crafting, which keep things nailed to their place, the walls and everything inside them upstanding, and the objects steadfast to the floor.

When he first gave me my gold kid slippers, we were in his room, and they gleamed and rustled out of the tissue paper, two lanterns casting their glow in the dark. They would be my companions, or so I thought, lighting my way through the fog which he would muster daily from powders as his way of greeting the dawn. He thought that his illness could be made to disappear in a cloud of smoke. 'Take them,' he said with special urgency, apparently as keen as I was for me to have something to lighten my tread. But as soon as I brought them back to this room, all their power seemed to vanish. Like me, they lose themselves against the sheen, cruel little pointers to how well I fit and I blend. Sometimes I sit here in the evenings, and as they slip off the ends of my feet, I curl and stiffen my toes inside them before they drop. My strength is not going, my resolve is not weakening, it is just being pushed, as they say, to extremes. I love to drape myself in accessories. Dresses, of course, but I have always cherished the extras most. Because they are dispensable, they have always struck me as the boldest statement of a woman's worth. But these slippers are different. Theirs is a far more intimate form of display. Over time, it came to feel as if the whole house deposited inside them its every mood. And whatever else, because they would never venture outside it, for both of us they meant that I was really living in his home.

Early every morning, before the light is fully up in the sky, I wash myself in the *cabinet de toilette* which adjoins his own. Between us, the slenderest partition hangs like a mist. My favourite place, it is the only room in his apartment which appears to have been prepared, not for some grey shade of another life, but for me. Three blue and white enamel jugs are set on the marble sink. In the balloon of their curves, they reflect the lilac of the walls and the glazed sapphire backs of the brushes which lie face-down on the surface, fine lines radiating out from their shining centres as though a stone had been thrown into a pool of bright blue. Two lights of frosted glass, perfect spheres, hang over the sink where I wash. All over the shelves and in the corners are tiny cut-glass bottles and porcelain containers, one of which – as if this were the place where she too can shed her indignation – Adèle fills daily with clusters of fresh red and pink and mauve flowers.

Often I hum to myself while I wash, and just sometimes, if I am sure he is listening, as I run the water down my back, over my breasts and my arms, I sing these lines from one of my favourite musical romances, Durand's *Binjou*:

> Sorrows are mad girls,
> Listen and you are madder still.

My stupid aunt had found it vulgar, and, wanting poetry of a rather different class, insisted in company that I sing in its place this line of Massenet:

A song of farewell arises from troubled springs.

But I was never troubled when we chatted through our partition, so slight that splashing in his sink sounded like water poured into mine. Nor, in these rare moments when I was happy to be his invisible spirit, was I saying farewell. Although I did want to warn him. We would drive each other mad, and him maddest of all, if he tried to rob me of the sorrows of my life and make them his own.

Across the hallway from the main door to my bedroom a long corridor stretches away from the body of the apartment into the furthest recesses of the building. Either it has not been repainted for a very long time, or else in the beginning, to mark the necessary distance of status in colour as well as length, it was plastered with a dull ashen grey. I have never wanted to venture along it, and am sure I would have been stopped if I had, but somewhere along this corridor are the domestic quarters where Adèle makes her home. For her this layout has the dreadful disadvantage that by the time she makes the journey to, and then back from, and to his room again, in response to some summons, as likely as not he will have changed his mind and made her effort pointless. But for us, since we could hear her heels on the parquet floor, louder it seemed than they need be – as if already prepared to be irked, she was concentrating her irritation in her feet – it has been a blessing. Not that she hasn't known what was going on. His home is her dominion and she has walked in to find me naked in his bed more than once. But it has given us the option of deciding on her behalf which shock to feed her, which outrage to enact for her benefit, while pretending to be fumbling in the dark. I would go red at my own conspiracy – today I am appalled at how much I have wanted to humiliate her and bring her down. My blushes served their turn. She thought she was exposing me. He thought he was protecting my modesty and shielding me from her affront.

After our return from the coast, we lived together in a kind of trance. Everybody, with kindness and discretion, quietly backed away. My aunt simply concurred, believing I am sure that this was the slightly unusual prelude to a betrothal which, she could now be confident, would be announced at any point. I even think that she had managed to convince herself, on no basis in experience whatsoever, that the unusual not to say improper nature of our arrangement could be relied on to produce the desired social outcome precisely because, with a boldness which would normally be considered to exclude it, we had reached the point of no return. And his mother left town to visit an elderly relative of his deceased grandmother, gathering around her the shades of the dead as the quietest reproach she could rally against the shame of the living.

She was incapable of cruelty and yet I sometimes wonder whether she took some pleasure in refusing me the solace of a maternal presence which, although she could not have imagined how much I longed for it, she knew – like everyone else – that I had never known. Perhaps she realised too, although consciously at least she would never have allowed such a calculation to cross her mind, that if she returned, however disapprovingly she might treat me, I would never go. As long as she stayed away, I could be relied on one way or another – under the soft pressure of her distant, silent, recrimination – to make my exit. During the whole time I have been here, she has visited only once, choosing with perfect timing a day when I stayed out longer than usual. I was pushing it – for my own purposes as I naïvely thought. No word about me passed between them, or so he said, but that evening, with a kind of studied idleness, he described to me how she had moved restlessly around the apartment, never stopping, flushed and wiping her forehead constantly with her hand, like someone trying to brush away a fly.

We had come straight from the station to his apartment, so my suitcases were abrim with summer, mostly frippery that could just pass for high elegance and so light that, when I lifted out my dresses, you could feel the coast trapped inside them as they slid, all sand and seaweed, through my hands. He made it his task to move me through the seasons. As autumn crept up on us, every garment for the outdoors would come courtesy of him. Always black and grey and brown, colours so discreet and fabrics so dense that you could lose your face in them, chinchilla fur on my head – he liked my toque best – and wrapped around my hands. He took advice, I could tell, and went to endless trouble. I only had to ask for the clothes of a duchess glimpsed in passing, my face pressed to the window, and they were mine. 'Did you see the Duchess of Clermont? Under her pelisse I could just make out her grey crêpe de Chine gown. She was wearing a stole of brushed dove-grey silk like you've never seen. Well, not exactly grey because, as she moved along, it turned the deepest blue.' A few days later, the stole appeared. I rushed to embrace him, threw it over my shoulders and, with the enthusiasm of a child who knows how to placate a parent before the first sign of anger, paraded up and down his room. I was displaying myself to his advantage. He was buying my time.

But if these gifts were to please me, they were also his way of licensing what was oddest and least acceptable about the life we shared. A belated form of etiquette, and a bargain in more than one sense of the term. The more gracious and elegant I became, the greater the wealth he packed about me, the more he could convince himself that he was offering his dues to a society which by now he more or less detested. I stepped out blazing a status and position which, as it happens, I would never gain. I would do him proud, while he sat at home all the while, quietly raging at my day. My clothes at least would bear his signature – my escorts, they were to accompany me out into the great wide world while shrouding me and deadening all the sounds.

So autumn and winter were for him. The heat of his apartment could be guaranteed to do the rest. When I returned in the evenings I would drop all my outside garments almost before I got through the door. And pick up breezily where I had left off, all air and transparency, muslins and silks and lace. Colours so pale, watery blue, rose, opal and mother-of-pearl, that they would draw any light, however weak, to their surface and make it shimmer and then multiply a thousandfold every time I moved. There was no need for any contact – he rarely left his room to greet me – he didn't even have to set eyes on me, but he had seen to it. He had got back his nymph from the seashore.

During the first few weeks, when I rarely went out, we started to pace each other into a rhythm so lulling, so natural as it came to seem, that it was almost invisible, the hardest thing for me to notice, let alone break. His rules were absolute and everyone in his household followed each one, however preposterous, without demur. At whatever point he awoke, a strange quiet, far more intense than the one which guarded his sleep, would spread like a mist through the apartment and circle protectively around me, and those who attended him, each in our separate rooms. We were the chosen children to his God and we would not die. No one would move until he rang on his bell, but we could all feel him biding his time, and we froze like puppets in a momentarily suspended play. I obeyed this rule happily, since I too like some things to be clear. But, unlike his servants, I relished it as a performance on which only I could draw the curtain, and for which one day I would be the one to take the final bow.

Once I was in his room, there was no stopping me. Ever since that first visit more than a year before this room had yielded to my touch. Far, far more than the one, arguably my own, with all its winning, pliant softness. Adèle would tread cautiously, screwing her eyes to meet the obscurity, straining with mute protest to avoid the dimly tantalising objects in her path. But I have blind sight. If there is one thing he has taught me, it is how to find my way in the dark. I could move about that room without seeing a thing, skirting any surface I wished to spare, chiding and humouring as I went. I could feel the weight of the room, which he had laid down on principle with such tenacity and devotion, lifting from his cramped and muffled chest. At the ends of his bed, vertical copper bars, rings strung out between them, wedged him in. Light flickered – barely – from the shafts which appeared to be growing from the back of his skull.

Under the shirt of his white pyjamas, just visible, a flash

of silk edging and shining buttons broke the flatness of his vest, thick Pyrenees wool, which he always ordered to the same design. A pile of them, together with the freshly laundered towels he insisted on, sat mounted, his silent attendants, on a small dark table by his side. The only other object, picked out in the glow cast by the green glass shade of his lamp, was a minute pair of crafted silver scissors with which devoutly, as though they were the pen and his hands the parchment, he sometimes manicured his nails. Mostly, he would lie there immobile watching me drift around before I would finally wind my way towards him and drop down, without let or hindrance or permission, on to his bed.

He never went out during the day. But at night sometimes, when he thought I was sleeping, I am sure he made his way back into his great grand world. I liked to think he had relinquished it, not out of his weakness, but for love of me. Even if the walls were closing around us. Even if it meant that the society I had believed he would throw open to me was retreating faster and faster, like a thief being chased through the sewers of the city who – whether by accident or to dazzle his pursuers – drops tiny glittering pieces of his hoard as he runs.

Once, when I was lying awake in the early morning at about six o'clock, I heard him let himself through the door and ring for Adèle. She responded so quickly she must have been waiting for his call. When they disappeared into his room, shutting the door behind him, I walked along the corridor past the trilby, white gloves and the black braided jacket which he had placed on the chair in the hall. I had heard her complimenting him on his elegance and his grace. 'Quite the lord, sir. If you don't mind me saying so.' He could alter his mood and even his gait to suit the occasion, holding himself in, almost bent, to save his strength and his breath, or pulling himself up to his full height on the back of his heels. According to his preferences, he had the body of a cripple or a king.

Outside his door I heard them laughing. He was regaling her with his tales. 'True the dress was stunning, some kind of silver and gold lamé, but imagine what she said when I complimented her: "It is the last money of France" – the wife of the Minister of Finance!' 'With the money of his second wife – a Rothschild of course – he had an enormous castle built just outside Saulieu and then as soon as she died he married an Italian princess. At least that keeps him off the back of Countess Greffulhe.' 'A dreadful marriage, I think he's violent, but you would never know. Exquisite, diaphanous, she conducts herself as though she were the happiest of women desiring nothing more than to bestow a share of her great happiness and good fortune on all around.' 'As for Count Pierre de Polignac, he has, in my view, dishonoured himself. Marrying the Duchess of Valentois, the natural daughter of the Prince of Monaco. True he acknowledged her and graced her with a title, but everyone knows her mother did his washing. The very idea – sacrificing his name to a laundry girl!' And then, without my being able to catch who it was, 'The only Jew – apart from the Rothschilds – to gain admittance to the Jockey Club.' 'You know, Adèle, I sometimes think that the nastiest are those who stare at themselves in the mirror and cannot forgive other people for being less ugly than they.'

After that, a long pause when I assumed he was lost in thought and she did not say a word. Talking to me, he often seemed to disappear from his own voice, as though he could walk away with half of himself, like a magician slipping off his head and carting it away under his arm. When he refocused, he would narrow his eyes and look surprised to find me – in silence and unflinching from a blow he had not cast – sitting on a chair or on his bed, or sometimes curled beneath him with my head resting against its deep blue counterpane.

I crept back to my room. I was not jealous. I didn't want to know any more. He talked to her because she had no claims. She had nothing to lose. Why shouldn't she hang on his every word? Lying back down on my bed, with my ears closed to him, I put my hands behind my head and listened to Paris rising to the dawn. Then I got up, pulled all my silk – camisoles, knickers and stockings – out from their drawers and placed them, carefully folded, ready to go – although I knew they would be stacked away again before the morning was past – in neat little shining piles over the floor.

There was something about our physical relations in those early days which I found oddly reassuring, even pacifying. Almost, I realise now, for the very reasons he had so vexed and puzzled me to begin with. 'We're not exactly lovers,' I once reproached him and then immediately bit my tongue. If he conceded the point it was out of concern for my reputation, but I never bothered about what was said. Slowly I had come to realise that what for some might be considered a failure was an opening. It gave all the other less likely forms of contact between us their chance. No ugly suspicions – not yet – had flooded our little moat. By encaging me, he had swept them all aside. And, because he had got rid of the world, he had stopped competing. Our bodies sank into the space. Little patches of intimacy would rise cautiously, to our surprise and almost to our amusement, from the deep. Not once during

126

that time did I feel invaded by him. When he caressed me, we were like two bodies just saved from drowning, gulping the same air. It took me a while to realise that we had gone too far back, that too much depended on it. Now I understand the trick question: 'Is it better to be nearly drowned or nearly saved?' Everything started to capsize from the moment it dawned on us more or less together – final irony that it could only be together – just how safe and easy we had become. I was drifting on a raft, storm over, sun burning gently into my face, and a shipwreck somewhere, so far behind me now that any notion of being rescued had dropped from my mind like a stone. But how unfair that the very peace and tenderness should come to mean that – unsparing of ourself and of the other, pulling ourselves apart into undreamed-of hostilities – we would have to beat our way free.

Odd as it may sound, his jealousy was then, as I see it now, his bungled attempt to save us both. Something had to be rammed back into the space which no longer existed between us. I knew immediately what was happening – I could feel the air splinter and its tiny pointed fragments collect about me – the moment I walked in the door. I don't think I have ever seen him look so relieved. 'I spoke to Andrée on the telephone. She is back in Paris and would be more than happy to accompany you. I can't, of course, because of my health, but you mustn't mind me. It is time you really got out and about.'

—

Andrée and I loved to walk the streets. We would sweep away from the dust and noise, which came at you as soon as you stepped out of his apartment, into the relative calm of the Boulevard Malesherbes. It wasn't really quiet – there was no less of a crowd – but because the avenue was wider you had the sensation of being cushioned from the blows. Pavements so broad, the air seemed to roll back the carriages. Huddled in the middle of the avenue, they looked like the reluctant entrants in a Roman chariot race. As you walked up towards the park, the sky touched the street in the distance on the brow of the hill. It must be one of the few points in the city where – like a child's first drawing before she knows any better – the sky hits the ground. From wherever we started, and whenever we started, beyond a certain point it was impossible to see. The future, as they say, was out of our hands. Even though we knew exactly where we were going. He couldn't have done this walk. It would have knocked him quite out. But he was always accompanying us in his way. That's what makes it so difficult. How can you triumph over someone who has never exactly made it to his feet?

Once in the park it was a different matter. Unlike the woods, where our friends liked to loiter, this was more of a family affair. There is something about the Parc Monceau, even the way its paths sweep round in slightly irregular curves, which makes everything in it seem accessible. Carefully tended lawns appear from nowhere, apparently to welcome the kind of people who couldn't possibly have anything to hide. Every time we lighted on an unexpected expanse of green, it felt as if we should immediately sit down to a family picnic. Regardless of whether we were accompanied by children, or the dampness of the grass. The glistening blades always looked moist in the sun. The mock forum which ran along the railings at the far end of the park seemed to be offering itself for encounters which would never take place. For every column there was a gaping hole of brightness, announcing that, however many turns you might take,

128

you would always, but always, be observed. Family life, I have realised — not of course that I know the first thing about it — is just such a bizzare combination of being more normal than normal, and then starting to wonder when you notice you are always being watched. As I looked at the children primly attached to their governesses, I could see that there was nothing here — the flowers did neat obeisance to the pavements — to give them any other ideas. Andrée and I straightened our backs and held up our parasols against the glare of the new spring. I was more elated than I can say to be back in her company. But our greatest joy was in finding, as we would every time we came to this park, that we were the only two unaccompanied young women to be seen.

On that first day, we wasted no time. Not surprisingly, she wanted to know what I thought I was doing. She didn't ask me straight out — she would never do that — but came at me, at her question, from round the side. We were sitting on a bench, moving our heads in unison from left to right, our eyes following the unruffled movements of the passers-by. Everyone looked as if they were in a lift moving sideways. A perfect distraction, since it made our conversation seem so much the less urgent and intense.

'Of course we've been wondering what you'd got up to. I haven't been worried, I wouldn't want you to think that,' she lied, 'I always assume you are fine.' I had often had occasion to marvel at the lengths Andrée would go to in order to sound like anyone other than her mother. Sometimes it gave the oddest impression that, instead of her speaking, a music box inside her was turning out the words from her mouth. But she had, as a result, the wonderful knack of sifting her own anxiety, as if she didn't really — although of course she did terribly — care. 'Don't you find it a bit stuffy?' She must have worked out what was going on, so I assumed she was referring to the suffocating heat of his apartment. But knowing Andrée as I did, and what passed for shocking in her eyes, I might of course have been wrong. Nothing he and I could do would ever remotely impress her. Maybe we did indeed look stuffy, like an old married couple of the servant classes, deaf to the world and only each other for company. As far as Andrée was concerned, ours – his and mine, that is – would always be a paltry affair.

When Andrée was in this kind of mood, I hardly had to say a word. It wasn't that I was fearful about giving anything away, it was more that she was staging an inquisition which neither of us believed in or had the slightest desire to pursue. I could already feel her mentally rehearsing their next meeting, placating him with the burnt-out offerings of our vacuous conversation – which she would fill out at the ready when required. What I said, how much I said, didn't matter. I could be sure that when she next saw him she would make up her answers, less talking than humming, as she went along.

Now I can see we were both the poorer for our loyalty. Our silence left so much, as was of course the intention, unsaid. It floated about us like a cloud halfway down the side of a hill. She was giving me all the room which, on the basis of our past loving, she knew I needed to love her again. And to free me from him. But it meant that everything that might have saved me, the very idea that I might need saving, was politely – she made it a point of the finest delicacy – dropped. So when finally she acted, it felt as though she was still – like she did at that moment – looking the other way. There was no one like Andrée for being pitiless at the merest hint of a fuss. I wanted no pity, of course. 'You don't have to tell me,' she lowered her voice slightly, although no one was listening, 'so long as you're all right. And,' she added just a little too promptly, 'don't you see, this way we can see each other much more. He's made us so – well, delightfully – correct.' With hardly an inch between us, we moved a little closer along the bench, patting and smoothing down our dresses even though they didn't have a single crease.

With what ease we fell back into our old, familiar pattern. All we needed was someone hovering somewhere who disapproved. We thought we were taking our chances and prided ourselves on our daring, as we had done so many times before. But I also remember a distinct sense, even on that first day and alongside the exhilaration, that my world was getting smaller. The difference between the two halves of my life, all of a sudden so reliant on each other, was starting to shrink. A perfect triangle. And I was the only one able to occupy all the points. Enviable, wouldn't you think? Something was turning nasty. Some-body, not quite any of the actors in the drama, was planning untold malice, somebody who would never get into the game. The sounds in the park got sharper. More wilful and pointed, the cries of the children raised their pitch. Seagulls squawked overhead. I was back with my little band racing and shrieking along the beach. We were playing hunt the ferret, holding and passing the ring over and over again as would only be possible in a dream. Each time I looked down, the person I thought I was passing it away from was standing in front of me, smiling with the ring held fast in his hands.

We got up and started to make our way out of the park, earlier than we had planned. Everything had become, for both of us I am sure, too full of itself. 'Let's go back,' she said. 'Maybe he won't be there.' I could feel her straining to rally our spirits and recapture our lost mood. As we sauntered along pretending not to hurry, she twisted herself towards me, leaning slightly at the waist although I am in fact the taller, like a grown-up trying to egg on a suddenly unco-operative child. Her grey eyes went darker, drawing up the gravel from the path. All their gentleness – how often had I felt Andrée's gentleness as the worse accusation – suddenly gone. The smooth, soft skin of an otter turning to flint. She was trying not to frown.

'Unlikely,' I replied, not to punish her but because I genuinely believed it to be the case. Except – the idea flashed up for a second – perhaps with an illness so fanned by attention, my absence might allow him too some kind of escape? Even if it was the last thing on his mind. Even if there was nothing he wanted less. My exit might have given him his cue. I knew how much – apart from his occasional sorties of the night – my being there rooted him to the spot. And how strange a calm descended over his apartment in the evenings when I returned after our embraces to my room. It wasn't that he no longer had any need of me – too obvious, too crude. No, my retiring to a place so within reach of him allowed his mind to let go. All he needed was a picture of me in place so he could, as and when the need arose, take it up and put it down at will. Then he didn't have to think about me any more. So maybe – I could hear my steps lighter on the pavement – with me out of the way in a shape he could hold fast to, since it was, as he believed, so wholly and cleverly orchestrated by him, he too would find himself obliged to take up his hat, call his carriage and go visiting, right in the middle of the day. I could see him, somewhat perplexed but proud at his new-found boldness, almost strutting – he never strutted – down the stairs. Putting the flesh on his obsessions. Fulfilling, despite himself, the spirit of the truth which was his greatest torment – that you never know what the other person is up to when you are not there.

As the idea started to grow on me, I allowed myself to be drawn on by the prospect, as exciting for me as I could be sure it would be, all too quickly, wretched for him. After the shortest reprieve. Could we get back before the delight had worn off, before – furious and with all his suspicions mounting – he rushed back scolding himself? If he was out, I could have Andrée in my room. Her very presence in that space would be enough to push back those walls. My Samson wreaking vengeance on the Philistines. We would sit there eating honey out of the carcass of a lion. We would blind ourselves, both of us willingly – after all wasn't that more or less the condition for entry into his apartment? – as the price to pay for bringing the whole building down about his ears. And for enjoying pleasures – I was suddenly overwhelmed with how long it had been – I had almost forgotten. But not quite. Without either of us having to sacrifice a single hair.

I think we were so dizzied by finding things as we had dreamt that we dropped all our cover. We knew he wasn't there before we were up the stairs. And the shock on the face of his housekeeper did the rest. She blanched with an indignation which grew by the minute as she struggled and failed to find a proper object for it to land on. It could hardly be me, since one way and another, all the more if he were absent, I was meant to be in her charge. But we shouldn't have been there without him. That was breaking all the rules. Far more, I could see, than my living there in the first place. As long as he was in his home calling on her services, she could bypass me. Swept along by the very weight and capriciousness of his demands. I smiled at her more kindly than perhaps ever before, or since. There we stood in bittersweet counterpoint, her bodice rising and falling with exasperation, mine with triumph and relief. There was absolutely nothing she could do.

Ask me which of us was the longer suffering: in fairness it would have to be Adèle. Although there is of course more than one way to measure suffering. On balance, I would say it was as deep as it was long. If I wanted to argue my own case. But she at least had the virtue of consistency. Although she misread me dreadfully, what made all the difference between us – about that much she was right – was that she had no designs for herself. Whereas, to the surprise of all three of us, I suddenly found myself stepped up a notch, a mistress flaunting her lover. With all the confidence of a kept woman who knows it is just a matter of time – after all, isn't the master dying? – before she inherits the home.

Andrée and I raised our arms behind our heads, took the pins out of our hats and hung them in the hallway. Not, in the normal run of things, something I did for myself. They sat on the rack at an angle, brims to the floor, feathers pointing upwards, like marionettes put away so brutishly at the end of the show that all their limbs are awry. Cheeky though, I thought, as we turned on our heels and made towards my room. 'We are not,' I said without so much as a glance over my shoulder, 'on any account to be disturbed.' I could feel the burden on her as she stood there, like a valet at a door through which too many people have arrived all at once, pulling himself together but barely able to take the strain of all the hats and canes and cloaks.

I wanted so much from that moment. I allowed myself

to forget almost everything I have ever learnt. I allowed myself to believe that all it would take – for what? – would be for us just to hold ourselves still and fast in that bright, shining room, like a top spinning silently on its thread. But, as I should have known by then, even quiet has its own echo. Listen long enough to the softest, lowest pitch, and you will hear it humming louder and louder until it starts to din. I was lulled by my first impression. To meet my expectation, all the heat of the apartment seemed to have fled, the currents rushing out – at the first sound of our footsteps – like rats between the boards. Taking the dust with them. Every day the tiny motes would be brushed away only to collect again within seconds. Over all the surfaces there would gather a layer of finest film, magnified in turn by the light which – I made sure of it – fell unobstructed into the room. The windows were never open, the balcony veiled, but I always pushed back the heavy gold brocade curtains as far as I could, drawing on the twisted braid cord with all my might. And then I would sit down and get up again to play with the nets. Pulling at the mesh and tucking it away – a bit showing? it shades things a little but then look how it diffuses and softens the light! Several times a day. Now that all the dust had gone, only the glare was left. The whole room glinted like a kitchen surface left to dry.

Andrée looked around her, blinking as if she had entered a fairy grotto. 'What on earth?' she didn't say it, but I could tell that, whatever she was thinking, it didn't quite chime in with my mood. I allowed myself a few seconds of believing I had performed a wondrous display of magic. Everything was shining so brightly that, for a moment, there was nothing to be seen. I too knew how to blind a lover.

We removed none of our clothes, not at first, but lay on the bed with our hands quietly moving, almost no pressure, inside each other's skirts. Anyone walking in would have to look twice to be sure. We were wholly at each other's disposal, but with all our coverings intact. Whether our eyes were shut or staring unblinking, there was nothing up for inspection. Nothing exposed. Just the bare silence of a room which wrapped itself, with perfect courtesy, around our concentration. Such thoughtfulness. Of all my lovers, Andrée is the only one I could call mindful. Not because she is especially skilled – I have had experience of women far more talented than her – but because she finds a way of holding the pitch of my excitement to one steady point. However much I am overtaken, something – some small piece of me, a piece she would never want to touch – stays behind. I think part of his problem is that he has never understood – no one has shown him – the kind of loving which knows how to drop its own claim. Take it and leave it, as you might say. Andrée does not want to swallow me. But nor does she want us to go scuttling back to our separate corners and then come out fighting, ready to go marching all over each other's domain.

By the time we took our clothes off and slipped between the sheets, we had so finely set our own tune that we had completely forgotten the risk. Who could know at what point he might burst in? Not into my room: he wouldn't do that, I don't think. But he would make sure we heard his entry, or at the very least the sound of his heels on the stairs, breaking and filling an absence by now appalling – he would assume or rather hope – to us both. Or I could be wrong. He might slink home and slip into his own room to wait silently for my return. And then sit there without us knowing, while the slow sounds of our pleasure made their way – one breath and then two and three – into his room. Like the noise of a child knocking louder and louder on the bedroom wall until, still with no answer, he cries out in the dark. The finest partition divided my room from his. He could be sitting listening to us now. Now we were lying head to toe, although going one at a time. I sat up, cupping Andrée's head in my hands, brought it closer towards me for a second, and then away so that her tongue was barely touching me at the end. Then I lifted her up quickly trying to stem and silence my own pace. All of a sudden, it was as if he were there watching, chin propped in his hand, one unruly mesh of hair falling, as it so often did, over his brow. A perfect, civilised, image of my own disarray. The tiniest bit ruffled. Just a touch miffed. His pleasure, not mine.

Andrée, always quick off the mark, heard him first and switched off all the lights. I pulled on his slippers and one of his favourite kimonos, the palest yellow silk with red embroidered flowers which now seemed too bold, almost garish. Like a cheap necklace, they picked out the flush on my cheeks. And, with no time to straighten my bed, I ran to his room, where I sat down at his desk. Andrée would field him. I had to find something else to do, something requiring the perfect mix of focus and inattention. By the pale glow of a solitary lamp, I lifted out a sheet of vellum and took his pen in my hand, dipping it into the ink and then holding it, for what seemed like an eternity, in the air. Only when I heard their raised voices in the stairway, although oddly it sounded as if hers were the greater protest, did I start to write. 'My dearest Aunt, I have been putting off this moment, but imagine my surprise. It seems that he has no intention of marrying me after all.'

Then the voices went quiet and I realised – it gave me the full measure of her fidelity – that, to give me as much time as possible, Andrée had managed to get well out of the door and to close it behind her before stopping and engaging him in conversation on the stairs. He had no key. He never did. The housekeeper had taken umbrage and, under pretext of some pressing errand, had gone out. To her mind, our love-making was aimed at her personally, and she would not stay to be insulted in her own home. So I would have to let him in. Obscurity never threw me, but I had never had to turn the lights on before and I fumbled for the switch in the dark. And then, before opening, I tidied my hair and tried to give myself the mildly troubled air of someone emerging from total absorption in a task. Inconvenienced perhaps, even distracted – I had of course not heard him until he rang the bell – but not, in no way physically, put out. By the time I had composed myself, I was confident that a woman of letters, not a lady of vice, was stepping forward to greet him at the door.

He was clutching a bunch of lilacs. Their bright purple swollen petals almost covered his face. As he lifted his head and raised an eyebrow quizzingly above the fronds, you would think that he – not I – was the one who had been caught in the act. He stood there clearing his throat. To me, he looked for all the world like a lover raising his head, partly for breath, partly curious and wanting – although fully aware that it is almost bound to blow the performance – to register his achievement on your face. The smell of the blossoms filled the stairwell. I hated the scent and he knew it, although I genuinely think he had forgotten. Until a few minutes ago. She must have been remonstrating on my behalf in the hope that he would take them away again and give me just that little bit more time. But as I stood there in front of him, barely dressed, covered from head to toe in deceit, all my irritation, and any slight vestiges of panic, filtered away. At a flick of a button, he still knew how to make me feel that all the danger was his. And, almost, grateful. I could only marvel at how much he was willing to suffer – his face was changing colour – to bring me his peace offering, the first and only true taste of spring ever to make it into his home.

He sat there, legs crossed, on his bed and quietly watched me as I finished writing my letter. Andrée was gone. I was, you could say, completely safe. But, although everyone had changed position, it felt oddly as if the previous scene was replaying, with him there staring exactly as I had imagined, just as I had pictured he would. The only sound was the scratching of the nib on the paper. I could see him grappling with reproaches which were rising, nameless and faceless, to his throat. But I also knew that if I kept my poise, and sat there long enough, he would subdue them. Because he knew that every time he challenged me, a little piece of me snapped off in front of him. And buried itself deep inside me, or else came to land – usually both together – right between his eyes. He didn't want to be flailing around, chasing dragonflies in the dark. We had lost the spirit. Neither of us was in the mood for a fight.

'So, dear Aunt,' I continued – I had told him I was writing to my aunt – 'I am quite dismayed. You know how much I value and trust your judgement. What, please advise me, should I do next? Your loving niece. Albertine.' I sealed the letter, put it down and walked over to his bed, letting my kimono fall open as I went. And then swung myself on top of him, rubbing myself – still wet from all that had gone before – back and forwards, back and forwards, over his thighs. I would leave him. I had taken the first step. But we still had a long way to go.

—

Tiredness crept into our lives on that day. Although his illness may have made him weary, even confined him to his bed, I don't think, before then, he or I had ever truly felt tired. Not as you would tell. Not in each other's company, at least. Languid perhaps, taking our time, sinking into our pleasures. Circling our suspicions, biding by our mistrust. But never tired. Or not the kind of tiredness – active, relentless – which so fills your head that any fatigue in your body seems an afterthought. This was a tiredness with a special energy, which trampled over everything and swept mean and silent and with the cruellest confidence into our lives. The kind of tiredness that pulls on every fibre in your brain till it stands rigid to attention, and then runs fine wire threads tight and fast between each one. I would tread up and down the lines like a rat on a trapeze. A dog, I was once told, who sniffs a bone on the other side of a high wall, will run at the wall where he smells his quarry, race a bit to the left and to the right but then, losing all confidence and all memory, will go back to where he started and hurl himself at the obstacle over and over again. Even if just a little further down on either side there is an opening which would deliver him his prize. He cannot carry in his mind the bone, and the scent of the bone, quite far enough. I threw myself against this tiredness with all my might. As I strained against it more and more, somewhere at the back of my mind, where the pathways still ran easy, I was only too aware that I was serving its purpose and not my own. Tiredness does not weary. Like those states of elation and despair which make you believe they will last to infinity – because they seem so devoted to you, they make you feel so chosen – once you are in there, you know that it will never stop.

Perhaps I was the one least prepared since, up until that time, tiredness had never been an enemy to me. There are advantages to being weary for a woman, as I am surely not the first to discover. You can let your body give as a way of giving nothing. It was something I had taught myself to do. Not just for my sake. Whenever we hated each other's presence and longed for a break neither of us knew how to ask for, I could use tiredness as my ambassador and graciously, without a move, take my leave of him while we were both of us still there.

Sometimes he would ask me for a sexual favour, and then, before I had had even the time, or so I thought, to register my hesitation, he would stop me and say – as if he was in fact the reluctant partner – 'No, it will make you tired.' Perhaps he never felt me more faithful than at moments like this, when my withdrawal from him and from the whole wide waking world was at his summons. But he didn't always make it so easy, or smooth the path so well. Then, if I didn't want him but felt I couldn't refuse, I would come to his bed and, as he leant towards me, just before he touched me, I would let myself go – like an understudy, one step ahead of the performance, rehearsing her part in the wings. Everything was in the timing. I would thwart his embrace by appearing, for the space of a second, to meet it all too gladly halfway. It always took him a few moments to register that my eagerness was a subterfuge. But he couldn't possibly misread me. I would lift my fatigue and, like mud to make me beautiful, spread it from my fingers all over my face.

Helpless in the face of this rival, he would be left grappling with the air, unravelling my weariness into his arms. So near and yet so far. Cruel? Perhaps, but then again perhaps not, since I have always believed that, when in doubt, nothing doing is fairest and best. Unless, of course – an idea I find growing on me now – you want to spoil things for ever.

Sometimes at the end of love-making, my body would go heavy with relief. Not out of pleasure, nor because it was over. But, having never quite lost track of how we started, our embraces – even when our greatest comfort – still carried the faintest traces of that first ordeal. Whenever we stopped, at whatever point we stopped, it was as if we were being granted a reprieve. So if there was anything punishing in what we asked of each other, it came only from our fear. For me, the hardest thing was getting up physically to leave. Each time I pulled myself from his bed to return to my own room, breaking the rhythm for the sake of a distance neither of us believed in, I felt I was being pummelled. As I drifted in a stupor across the corridor, arms suddenly appeared out of nowhere, clinging to me from the walls. With every step I took, it got worse. By the time I got to my room, my head and every limb of my body would hurt. He had dispatched me, but he would not let me go. Once he was safely shot of me, he could hand himself over to an anger for which he had neither body, nor world, nor time, and rain down on me with blows.

But everything changed on the day I wrote my letter. Now he didn't want me to leave. From then on he never would. Once or twice, with a gesture as grandiose as it was unconvincing, he suggested we part, showed me the door as one might say. But although he allowed himself to imagine a life quite without me, as long as I was in his house he would wrap himself around me, fold upon fold, like a winter cape on which a tailor expends all his fabric, first to flaunt his abundance, for the sheer luxury of such excess, and then because he simply can't stop. Nothing, not even tiredness, was ever to come between us again. So if it weighs down so hard and mercilessly on us now, I am sure it is because it is shaping its temper to ours. No let-up. No slack. Once he made his decision, he needed me there constantly and never more than at the very moment when in the past he had been keenest to push me away. He was taking back the night and his vigil would be permanent. Even if, like a mother hovering over a dying child, he would not sleep. For some reason he thought I could. He made it his passion. It became his burden and most fervent belief. He only had to lie there, limbs aching with a fatigue for which there would be no solace, and the sleep which never came to him would pass to me as a gift. His last will and testament. If he only knew. Without either one of us realising, at least not to begin with, we have become rivals – perhaps the fiercest rivals – over sleep.

Imagine two children, a brother and sister who have promised their irate mother, on her umpteenth night-time visit to their room, to stop talking. Two children pretending – to her but also as it happens to each other – to be asleep. Both trying not to breathe in the mistaken belief, which perhaps only a child would hold, that another person breathing close by, instead of rhyming and soothing a sleeper, will wake her up. But if you don't breathe, sooner or later you will gasp. Our task got harder and harder with every second that ticked away. We were locked in a battle of wills with no possible winner since the first one to break the spell and sit up to claim victory

143

would immediately be admitting defeat. How on earth did we devise such a perfect struggle, more eloquent than either of us could have ever dreamt? Look at how two people sleep together. It will tell you more about what is happening between them than anything else.

I had kicked off my slippers and trailed my kimono over the back of one of his armchairs before lying down on the bed. He stood up and walked away, hugging, almost slapping, his arms round his chest. Our encounter was already going sour on him and if he didn't hold on to himself fast, all the warmth would escape. Another one of those moments which was rebounding against us even before it was done; when the sky would move for a second and then come pressing down on to the floor. We faced each other trembling, the murmur of our bodies still echoing together across the room. But how could we possibly know – the sounds are so similar – whether the soft, slow throb was the faint, delicious residue of what had just passed between us, or whether our limbs, long before thought could focus, were already attuned, jangling, to the whole sweep of recriminations to come?

I would do anything to avoid his rage. As would he. But the more he muffled his fury deep inside him, the more fiercely it got to me. I wanted to be back in our hotel room. There the mere presence of the light from the sea diffused us, whatever pass we had reached. I don't know why people have ever thought that holding oneself back spares anyone. A storm that plays itself out and sweeps wide and clear may bruise the landscape through which it travels. But it does not destroy it, crush the vegetation and rip up the trees, like a hurricane which waits, draws breath close to the earth, and then spreads out its shoulders across the whole expanse of the sky. I

144

watched him struggle, as I had so many times before, and could see the clouds rising, hear the slow hiss of gas, the lid moving under a thumb pushing hard and powerless – because of its very own pressure over time – to stop it. 'I will be back in a minute,' he said. Anger would not draw us together this time. I shivered and slid under his bedclothes. But, reluctant as I am to admit it, I knew that I was less frightened than him.

The only thing to do was to play dead. If you lie there still enough after a battle, so I have been told, they won't shoot. They will leave you for the other side to pick up later, while they go looking for someone else on whom they can use their toys. I would have to be careful though, or even that might set him off prying around to see who had been there – even if they had killed me – before him. I felt my body go limp. Before the first tremors were through me, I recognised it for the old and familiar friend who, instead of letting me sleep, would paw at me, coaxing and irresistible, like a sensuous, nagging, child. I closed my eyes and didn't move. And then pleaded, as I so often do to someone or something inside myself, that no images would come rushing into my head. That my mind, like my body which lay there like a possum faking, would go empty and quiet and still.

A jealous man never sees – perhaps I should have told him – that his greatest rivals are not a woman's other lovers, who after all make room for him and who come and go as she, and they, may please, but her other companions of the night, who always arrive when they are least welcome and crowd every last corner of her mind. I would lie there ransacking the furniture of the dark and then, convinced this was how best to keep out my private intruders, tidying and sweeping up the dust. I would set the whole world on its heels to be rid of them. But they craved and thrived on my attention. Why did I never have a mother to tell me that the more, tearful and sleepless, I begged and remonstrated against them, the more reluctant they would ever be to go? If only I could sleep – I knew I was setting the cart before the horse – they would surely leave me alone.

I felt his presence back in the room. He was standing by the door waiting to see if I was asleep. And then, if I was, to see whether this would be enough to spare us both. Far more tense, and more immobile, if that is possible, than I was. Steady and alert to the faintest sound, we were searching in opposite directions over the same ground. He could only be sure if I didn't move, I would only feel safe when he did. As he walked towards me, I started to breathe. Even for me, if by no means the real thing, it was a fair imitation of sleep. So you see, as I once said to my aunt, I do owe him a lot. Not quite better the devil you know. But better by far the one who sits beside me wrapped in his delusion, than the one who knows all there is to know about me, and has no other habitat, because I made him up all by myself. He thought I had another self inside me, a woman who truly would be the answer to his dreams. I wanted to shout out: there is someone else here. But you wouldn't want her. Our organs are too tightly sewn together. We will strangle each other before long. Call the doctor to sever the twins.

Sometimes, instead of coming from inside, it would be the world outside that loomed up in front of me barricading me against sleep. A shadow standing out against the dark. When I pierced my eyes against the night to see better, it would break up into tiny specks which would start to move and drift apart. A convoy of birds wheeling round for one last word before migrating. I could hear them chattering to themselves. They were there to proclaim their freedom. We are out of here. We have far better things to do than to spend the night in your dreams.

If you cannot sleep, they say, move through your body, muscle after muscle, limb by limb, and tell each one, without passing on until it has obeyed you, to let go. Not exactly an order. We are not back at the *lycée*. But firmly enough for your body to brook no argument. A pleasure, in fact. A bit like sex with my first companion, without the final rush. Or, as if you were a novice, grateful she is about to leave the trials of the world behind her, willingly receiving her first instructions from a nun. And breathe slowly and deeply; imagine you are a fish at the bottom of the sea, never taking a second breath until the bubbles from the one before have risen all the way up to the surface from the deep. Even if you are not sleeping, these rhythms mark a tempo which is so much its own that it leaves you completely out of time. He had been staring at me, lost in his thoughts, for what seemed like ages. Solitary watcher, as he imagined. The web of his concentration closed round me like a net. All words put out. Now there could be no rejoinder. I will confess anything, I thought as I lay there, but never this. Then, as he stretched out alongside me, his breathing started to move in tune to mine. He was the one ostensibly awake, but I was the one testing his dream.

I moved my legs, curled them further beneath me, and then moved again to let one of them trail close by him on the bed. Not too still, I thought. He won't believe it. I wiped a strand of hair from my face which, even though my eyes were as good as closed, was blotting a patch of

147

him from my vision. How bizarre that, wanting above all else to evade and deceive him, my fiercest desire became to reach him without obstruction, to see, feel and touch every part of him as closely as I possibly could. We had found the only way left for us to be together. Now I was the invisible maestro, I didn't mind – it was the last time I wouldn't – whatever he did.

He lifted my head, laid me back on the bolster, pressed his mouth against my lips for a second, wound my arms around his neck. I have never felt as loved by him as this. With neither planning nor foresight, I had succeeded – or had we succeeded between us? – in lifting away everything we had ever struggled against. As I went limp in his arms, part of me was watching the whole scene unfold, but now nothing about it was feigned. I would die for this sleep that was not really sleep. He would nurse me all the way to my tomb.

Then he placed his leg alongside mine and started to stir gently against it. My hand inside the bedclothes, clasped fast between my thighs, picked up a rhythm which was all his. Something like this had happened before, I remembered, the very first time in this room. But then we had not managed – I wonder if a man and woman ever quite manage this one together – to be there so wholly for each other. Quietly, without a glimmer of consciousness passing between us, I took myself away and handed him back to himself. 'You do not need me,' I wasn't pleading, that voice had gone silent, I was just telling him, 'you do not need me any more.'

He got up and stood staring at my kimono on the chair. Just for a while it seemed as if he was going to pick it up and slide it over his skin. Crush it. Let the silk, so light it is almost invisible, take the stain away. How can you possibly do violence to a fabric which so willingly crumples in your hands? A kimono holds no secrets. Or if it does, it carries them like cobwebs hanging in the wind. It lay there arms akimbo, flesh gently ruffled, almost shrugging, a body without a head that doesn't care. No offence. None intended. You won't find anything here. He hesitated, walked away and then back again, looking from the bed and back to the chair as if it held the last vestige of his obsession, the relic of his belief, which he never completely abandoned, that somehow or other, in some time and place neither of us had ever come to, he would finally possess me. I sat up, my eyes widening slowly against the night. I was still grasping at the faint shape of sleep. And then, a little confused – but comforted, untroubled, as if making out the silhouettes – I opened my arms to the whole room and called out his name.

About three o'clock in the afternoon a week later, we set off for the house of Mlle Léa. Andrée was once again, after the briefest intermission, my chaperone. He sent her out by my side armed with his instructions, like an apprentice servant being tested to see if she would come back with his favourite chocolates, which he would barely touch, or with the red and white silk waistcoat which he had once ordered but then never worn. Whatever he imagined as having passed between Andrée and me had ceased to torment him. Or so it appeared. He wasn't indifferent. He seemed to think that the tables had been turned. We could be as close as we liked, do whatever we liked, the more she moulded herself to me the better. His shadow. And my familiar, bending with my every move like flesh stuck fast to the bone.

We made our way across the city with steady and

unaccustomed resolve. Without any need for discussion, we both knew exactly where we had to go next. His apartment had not served us. Its welcome, so obliging, so cloying, had been a decoy. Like a wind which suddenly changes direction, it had thrown us together and then wrenched us apart so brutally, there may as well – at least after it was all over – have been no difference between the two. More than anything I wanted to breathe my own air. To be out in the open. Close to water. Not the sea this time, but a river. Water that flowed. And not out of taps, as it did in his apartment, gushing and spluttering like oil bursting livid from the earth. My aunt had a country house by the river which she used rarely when I was a child but had now started to occupy – before the season was upon us – in the early summer months of the year. Because I hardly knew it, I could paint it whichever way I pleased. In my mind's eye, I pictured a building like the forum in the park, with nothing but open spaces, as if the vistas you normally expect to see from a house window could turn around, sweep up the pathway and in through the front door. In the meantime, Mlle Léa would do. Nicely, as it happens. She would receive us, we could be sure, offer us sanctuary. Her small tangled house, vines knotted over its face, was set back from the street to the north of the city near the Sacré Cœur. We headed off, clinging to each other, two orphans searching for a home in a storm.

At home, reclining on her ottoman, Mlle Léa could have been posing for a portrait. She was covered almost from head to toe in a beige satin gown, which creased its way down from her chin to the floor, where it flowed over the carpet like froth on boiling cream. Trimmed at her neck and around her feet with ivory-coloured fur, the rest of the gown clung to the contours of her body, as if party to a silent agreement that only the far extremities of her body were in need of being dressed. One leg crossed over the other, her raised thigh stretched along the divan like an alabaster carving, or a pillar of an ancient temple which had fallen, impossibly intact, on to its side. Her hair was pulled back in a chignon, but now, instead of being stretched back taut from her brow, a dark thick fringe came down over her eyes. Her face was almost powdered away, just a splash of vermilion on her mouth. It picked out the divan, which was crimson velvet, icing on a pool of blood. She slid over its surface. Terror was beneath her. A gesture. Something whose audience she courted and played to, and then just as graciously disowned. Inside the house of Mlle Léa you could let yourself go because she ruled it with a will of iron. Since my passage here would be brief, I knew I was secure enough – for once I need not be frightened – to fall into my own fear.

On one side of the train of her dress, a red setter with its patches of amber and white fur and long pointed snout, lying in a curve which perfectly matched the sweep of her gown in reverse, crescent moons back to back, sharing the same animal nature; on the other Esther Levy on the floor against the divan, legs curled under, kneeling like a page-boy while she combed her fingers through the feather fan which Mlle Léa was dangling on her lap. With her free hand, Mlle Léa was stroking her dog. As if a *demi-mondaine* walking the boulevards in the middle of a freezing winter day suddenly decided to take off one of her gloves and, in search of a warmth which had instantly escaped from her uncovered fingers, started fondling her muff. To this ritual all the parties brought their utmost concentration, while managing at the same time to look casual, if a little remote and even bemused. A slight strain to her features suggested that Esther might be less than enraptured by her own show. An aspidistra hung its huge leaves over the whole scene. Esther's hair fell in a coil to her shoulders. She got up – Mlle Léa seemed barely to notice – and walked towards us as soon as we came into the room.

She led us to a far corner, where we sat down on three chintz-covered chairs. 'Albertine,' she said in a voice whose concern, out of respect for her paramour, was muted by her commitment to pleasure, 'what a delight.' She lent forward on her chair on the verge – I am sure – of asking for my news or my plans. I then watched as both forms of curiosity, the most natural as you might think in the world, dropped unspoken from her lips. Esther knew all there was to know about silence. She was discreet, not because of the scandal of her own position which, although as public and brazen as mine was private, had an odd symmetry with my own. But because she understood that the smallest piece of my past, even the tiny fragment of the day which had led up to this moment, as soon as it was gone, was gone and fell back into a blur. And, far more than I did, that the future I was steadily beckoning and willing into being was completely out of my hands.

We stayed chatting for some time, oblivious to the figures who passed in and out of the room. Apart from a lamplight which beamed straight on to Mlle Léa, picking her out like the most important prop on the stage, the lighting was so subdued that you could barely make out who they were. Mlle Léa glowed as she always did, casting her audience into the shadows. In fact we weren't interested in the company. As they drifted through, the dull murmur of their conversation was a perfect backdrop to ours. It gave what we were saying to each other an added cushion in a room already bedecked with giant cushions of heavy tapestries embossed with strange flowers, and throws, with fringes like creepers, which were scattered all over the floor. Not for people to sit on – no one lost their composure or descended so low – but as blandishments, the soft reminders of the unlimited acts which Mlle Léa always encouraged her visitors to indulge in elsewhere in her home behind closed doors.

Sitting there, I felt she was staging for my benefit a little rehearsal, light relief of a sort. You dropped your guard here. But you would be wrong to think it was an unlived life you were being given permission and freedom to perform. Step through this door, and it was the unspoken part of the life you were already living which came rushing out from the wings. Together he and I, day after day, would press our heels down hard on the pain of what we were doing to each other. I had received the favours of Mlle Léa before. She had given me solace with no price. But now I was after something else. As much as I desired to escape from him, I wanted the world to appreciate just how much – however dreadful – we were capable of. It was time to lift the covers from his bed. So this is why people go courting disaster, not blind and foolhardy, but because once you have reached a certain pass, disaster starts to look like a friend. You need somewhere, my child, where no one is pretending. Mlle Léa wafted her message across to me from the divan. In this house the beast never sleeps.

As Esther and Andrée sat talking, heads bowed towards each other, hands clasped across their laps like two schoolgirls reunited after the holidays, I started to look around the room. In one of the corners, a lady visibly older than the rest of the company was holding court in her own small way. Although the room was dark, I could see the lines etched on her face, its pallor beneath the rouge, the droop of her eyes, and the stiffness of her poise as she straightened her back against all her body's urges, more taut and rigid than a saluting cavalier. She was dressed in black, a gown of black taffeta which stretched out almost horizontally on all sides and then dropped suddenly to the floor, as if she had stood up at the theatre and walked out still encased in her box. A pleated collar pointed upwards and cast shadows around the lower half of her face. You could hear her skirts rustle and creak above the muffled voices in the room. Only the dress – out of deference to the decrepitude of the body under-neath – was allowed to ache. In her outstretched arm, she held a black walking cane with a tiny ivory carving on its head, which captured the light of a small Dresden lamp by her side. I could just make out the shape of a naked woman on her back, legs slightly apart, with one knee pointing in the air, polished to perfection – no knee was ever so smooth – by the ministrations of the lady who sat there caressing and rubbing on the handle as she spoke. She was manifestly somebody's patron. But she was also there for the sheer pleasure of being in a world where it had been silently agreed that pleasure – however betrayed by the age of the body still in search of it – would never cease.

Esther had got up and gone back to Mlle Léa. She was undoubtedly her servant, always the younger sister, always aiming to please. We had more in common than I had first thought. She pandered to Mlle Léa in order to protect her, and herself at one remove, from her own wrath. I had gone from the house of a man whose body would not

154

serve him, to that of a woman who was flawless and for whom the whole world, inside or outside the theatre, was a stage. But for that very reason Mlle Léa had far more to lose. The old lady was present as part of her unbounded generosity – let her enjoy herself as she will – but also as token, mascot, prop, poodle and warning from the gods. A little concession granted, with the utmost kindness of course, all the better to be ignored. As long as the younger woman was there to indulge her, Mlle Léa could go easy. She would never have to consider the possibility that the mastery she exerted over her body and her life were a fraud. Her honesty only went so far. Her motives as pure as they were corrupt. At the house of Mlle Léa things came out into the open, but on one condition. Notwith-standing the old lady in the corner, things had to be seen – they still had to have a body wanting to be seen – to be done.

Into this house, then, came the misfits of Bohemia, the misfits of the misfits as one might say. They did not necessarily belong to the world of the artiste, but each and every one of them, with an urgency in no sense diminished by their love of performance, had something vital to stage. Two young women playing cards in a corner leant over the table so far that, without touching, they had to be breathing each other's breath. And then underneath the table, I could see their feet search each other's out, their ankles twist together and then stiffen into a lock. They were holding something back for later – no vulgarity would abuse the hospitality of their hostess – but they had already passed beyond the end and into torment before they had even begun.

Esther, who had rejoined us, saw me watching them and leant over to explain. 'The one on the left is very rich and was married off far too young. The other was her private governess when she was still – although of course she still is – a girl. They are always getting into a scrape of one kind or another. Flaunting each other in public as if they want nothing more than to be discovered and then coming here to hide. But they always seem angry with each other. Even though they have got away from her parents and husband, they still insist on getting into a fix.' I looked again. Above the table these two souls deftly took hold of the prohibition against them and turned its constraint into bliss. Underneath their far more urgent and direct passion obeyed the curse of the elders – no good will come of this. But you would be hard pushed to say for which half of their bodies, upper or lower, the pleasure was more intense.

By now Esther was watching me very closely. She knew of my occasional relations with her lover. But this time it seemed as if she had a further reason to be intrigued. Ever since the night of the ball, she had been aware of my other attachment. But unlike Andrée, for whom he was an obstacle as great as he was ultimately irrelevant, Esther wanted to find a place for him amongst us. Not literally. That was out of the question. No less than Andrée, Esther wanted the house of Mlle Léa to be somewhere to which I could escape. But for her escape had a different meaning. Less cloak and dagger. Less freedom to roam. Fewer walls without walls. Something like an inner refuge where, far from fleeing anything at all, there would be nothing, which must mean including him, I would not feel able to embrace. Esther wanted me to risk more. She had the greed – although greed is not quite the right word, certainly not greed like my aunt's, let's say she had the breadth – of her own convictions.

In the far corner of the room a sofa of smooth damask silk was set expectantly along the wall. Arms puffed with fabric protruded from the side and then curled and bent, suddenly naked wood, down to the seat. Pointed wooden legs tapered to the floor and pinned themselves almost gingerly to the carpet, like compasses trying to steady themselves against a trembling hand. Pink satin cushions with black brocade were propped neatly to the back of the sofa, seemingly on the lookout for customers. In front were two pouffes, one sleek velvet cream pulled taut over the surface, the other plushly upholstered black with silk grey tassels dangling from the base. One naked, one dressed. Together the three pieces sat there waiting. As if someone was invisibly drumming their fingers on the upholstery. What next?

Esther stood up, took me by the hand and led me over to the sofa. I sat down and lay back at her bidding, as it felt, although she had done very little. She had the kind of authority which never needs to impose what it wants upon the world around it. Not calm, as if the idea of forcing calm were not the most flagrant nonsense, definitely not order, nor indeed anything else. Docile he thought me, I was as docile in her hands as I would ever get. She was halfway between a nurse and a procuress. As she gently urged me on to the body of the sofa, I stretched my arms out behind my head, raised a knee and arched my back against the sides. It took me a moment or two to realise that I was slowly prostrating myself like the ivory figure on the end of the old lady's walking stick.

Seated on the black upholstery pouffe beside me, she then lifted my ankles and, as if it were the most natural thing in the world, slipped my shoes from my feet. I loved these shoes. Pointed ivory satin, with the minutest steel beads cascading down the front which shook as I walked, they were cut so low over my feet that, through my stockings, you could make out the faint lines between my toes. Whenever I wore them, I felt as if I was displaying my finest riches while also declaring that the path to what they so imperfectly covered – and from there to the rest of me – lay open and easy and sweet. I stretched my toes just for a second as I took in the slight flow of the air. From the other side of the room, I could feel Mlle Léa's glance upon us. She nodded half-smiling at Esther, granting her approval with a mixture of caution and good grace.

Andrée was now sitting next to us on the cream pouffe. She got up and made a place for herself by my side. With one hand I pulled her head down on to my chest, with the other I gently – you would only see it if you were right up as close as Esther – pulled back, just a fraction, the end of my skirts. Esther wrapped her hand around my ankle and, dropping her head towards me, started – with tiny fast flickering embraces – kissing the ends of my feet. Like Louis XIV in his annual ceremony to commemorate the Last Supper, stooping to bathe and kiss the feet of thirteen children of the poor.

My tongue moved over Andrée's ear while she bit, gently, firmly, but never too much, at the exposed skin of my throat. 'How divine,' I said, addressing both of my girls, as they now seemed to me, at the same time. I could feel Mlle Leá's eyes still upon us. She was not guiding – Esther was guiding – but she was undoubtedly part of the scene. As we three increased our pace and moved, within the bounds of discretion, further along the avenues we had opened, the faintest tremors started passing between us, from one to the other, limb to limb. I remembered my days on the beach with my little band, although this was a

158

new kind of pleasure – less showy and pushy, no longer at sea – which knew how to grow, to mature, through its own restraint. We were covered by the dullness of the light. But also by our own movements, as careful as they were minute. Above all, we were still observing the decorum of Mlle Léa's drawing room.

It didn't last. With a fury that came from and carried me somewhere I have never been before, I drew back my heel and lashed out, kicked hard against Esther's face and clasped my arm around Andrée's neck so she could hardly breathe. Who were we trying to fool? Gentleness such as this, which I had fled to more than once one way and another, was a hoax. Esther had been right that you can always make room for more. There will always be more experience, more room, as one might say, on the bed. But I do not know to this day whether what pushed itself against my gullet, blocking my throat, rolling my tongue back inside my skull, was part of her promise. Just how generous can anyone get? My early triangle with my first lover flashed before my eyes, pain as exquisite as it was raw, like a poodle half permed and half shaved. Why, when people talk of refining torture, do they never consider what exactly is being, or rather failing to be, refined? Let's dance, a voice was singing inside me, you can take it, unlike him, you can both of you take it, let's really dance.

Do not ask me why it happened. Anger such as that arrives without warning, bearing no instructions, then turns hard on its heels and is gone. It is anger, not pain, which is most canny at tearing away all words and all memory, at taking its own breath away. So I do not remember whether it ended because they broke free of me, whether I stopped myself or whether, miraculously, they were able to seize on my anger – I was now trembling with rage – and muffle it back into our embrace. Then suddenly I noticed that somebody was watching. It wasn't Mlle Léa unless, unbelievably, she had stepped off her divan and out of her favourite role, rupturing the harmony of a room which so wholly depended on her, and walked over to where we lay. She wouldn't do it, I was sure. However shocked, she would, as the surest way to restore the balance, treat any such moment as a passing tantrum and simply avert her gaze. Children! And then again, it was exactly what she wanted. Although she would never let herself slip, not for one second, she measured her own integrity by how much her guests gave away.

Out of the corner of my eye I could glimpse whiteness. Someone bathed in a glow which had nothing to do with staging or spotlights, but possessing its own distinctive and no less artificial brand of charm. It was a man silhouetted in the dazzling light of his own profile. Watching, as intoxicated by the spectacle being played out before him as he was horrified, Octave stood there. Frozen far beyond the famously rigid posture which, even in the best of circumstances, normally glued him to his place. Octave nearly always looked embarrassed. It suited him. But he would happily sacrifice his own nature and fumble his way into ease to rescue the day before him. Almost apologetically he was offering himself as my saviour, as he had of course done before, rushing on to the scene unannounced and, although I didn't realise it then, for one last time.

Andrée and Esther huddled together on the sofa while I went across to Mlle Léa. To pay my respects. Not what she normally wanted. She lowered the lids of her eyes. She had served her turn. We both knew we wouldn't see each other again. Octave put his cape, hat and gloves on the black pouffe and sat down on the velvet one alongside. The two girls adjusted themselves in response. Then the three of them – facing each other in the corner – bent their heads together and started making their plans.

—

Each morning Louis XIV was wakened by his head valet, who slept fully clothed at the foot of His Majesty's bed. The chief physician, who was also always present when he dined, and the chief surgeon, along with the King's nurse, all entered his bedroom at the same time. The nurse would kiss him while the others rubbed him, often changing his nightshirt, as he was subject to sweats. After fifteen minutes the grand chamberlain was called or, in his absence, the chief lord-in-waiting of the year, and with them the main officials, one of whom opened the curtains and presented holy water from the holy basin near the bed together with the book of the Office of the Holy Spirit. Surrounded by all his attendants, the King would lead the way into the Council Chambers for the first service before he had even been handed his dressing gown.

He was preoccupied by morbid subjects. Details of operations, illnesses, anatomy and the question of where he was to be buried were favourite topics of conversation, even with the ladies, who had to conceal an embarrassment they shared with the rest of the court. About his own condition and diseases he was invariably pessimistic. Several times a day he would go to check the temperature on the crystal thermometer attached to a window of the Apollo Room, where a throne of crimson damask, which he never used, was raised on a daïs. As would his footman at least three times every day. Perhaps he thought that, though he himself was bound to die, if the temperature of the throne room held steady, the glories of his country and empire, which were of course all his glories, might be spared. On his dogs he lavished the most extraordinary amount of attention – he had five or six packs whose hunting, resting and walking were organised to the finest detail, in tune with, or even exceeding, the rest of the court. According to the journal of the Marquis d'Argenson, the King devoted himself more assiduously to his dogs than he did to managing the wars and finances of France.

I had first visited Versailles as a young girl with my aunt. I think she wanted to take me there, not so much to gawk at the riches, as to impress upon me that there were worlds where a diplomat breathed the same air, lived under the same roof, as a king. Where someone of our – or rather her – class, however far they travelled along the points of the compass, would always gravitate back to their place under the still, steadfast, rays of the sun. When the King went to the Cabinet after his morning ablutions and prayers, the only ones to stay behind were his bastard sons and their tutors who, like the house valets and builders, had entered not through the bedchamber but from the hall behind. My aunt of course was not concerned with such niceties if indeed, even out of concern for me, she noticed them at all. But, contrary to her intentions and despite the pleasure she took in our visits, the first thing I learnt from the Château of Versailles – my very first history lesson you might call it – was that it is not altogether clear in this world whether it is better to be a bastard or a dog.

My aunt loved the precision. 'Rules,' she would repeat as she guided me round the palace, 'rules, my dear. There is nothing you can't do with the correct rules. Believe me, I know.' She once made me stand for what felt like an inordinately tedious length of time waiting for the hour to change on the famous astronomical clock of Louis XV, which not only displayed the hours and years and months but the lunar phases and cycles of the planets. Apparently on New Year's Eve that King would sit in front of it and refuse to be moved until he had witnessed the clock complete the revolution of the year. But her favourite was the Victory clock of Louis XIV, less sophisticated – its technology long surpassed – but far more crudely to the point. On the hour roosters crowed and flapped their wings and Louis XIV emerged out of a temple with Victory in a cloud, who would crown him to the sound of a carillon. Since, as history has proven several times, a monarch cannot be confident he will be monarch for his lifetime, she must have thought it only the most royal of common sense to make sure you were crowned more than once.

In her own way, by ushering me around so earnestly, she was also trying to be generous to us both. You can belong here, if only you try hard enough. Simply by taking me in she had added to her own vulgarity, and to the slight but constant jolts of her social position, the terror of the totally unknown. In its days of glory Versailles was always damp, the castle sitting above a marshland, whose waters close to the surface fed the hundreds of evergreens in the grounds. Their roots were too weak to go in search of the deeper moisture of the earth. Planted for constancy, for the blaze of green they shot forth throughout the year, but resting on nothing, they quivered and fell at the merest hint of a storm.

I had my day at Versailles when he sent me off a few months back, accompanied by his chauffeur. Today it seems light years away, like a piece of star dust which has parted from its orbit in the night sky, although even as I sit here the gap between then and now is starting to shut. When he made the suggestion, I was not wholly surprised. One way or another, it seems to have been part of the educational hopes of those who have made my life their project that I should take in the lessons of Versailles. For her that I would imbibe the appropriate forms of decorum. Subdue my fervour to the court. Learn to serve. But while you may think this too would be his intention, my obedience was not his aim. Majestic he was in the fuss he produced all around him. Tyrannical through his illness, tyrannical because, as Versailles also teaches, it is the prerogative of the powerful – the most fervent wish of kings and princes – to be treated like a petulant and feverish child. But from all of this he has always done his best to protect me. Unlike her, he has never ever wanted me to fawn.

Nor, although I was in many ways his most prized possession, has he sought to put me on display. His little experiment. Ownership the more pure and absolute for never announcing itself to the world. All the riches of Versailles were there to declare to me what a price he must be paying, how deeply worthwhile our life together must be – how he must love me – if he was not blazing his most valuable of all valuables from one end to the other of his castle walls. I would notice the contrast. He would gain my respect. While he could rest assured that I was coveting the opulence – this he did want, I am certain – and, like all the poor people who milled to the castle, being roused to no end of excitement by the wealth.

'It will interest you,' he said as he sent me off, ever eager for me to educate myself, like a monarch keen for the improvement of his people, on condition that they never direct the fruits of their knowledge at his own head.

He never dreamt that I might have been to the palace before, lapping up the details, giving myself a royal education of my own. Learning fit for a queen. There for the taking for anyone who visits Versailles.

As soon as we arrived, I dismissed the chauffeur. He had come, I knew, to spy on me. And to spy on me, even at a distance, he would surely do everything he possibly could. He was, after all, in his master's pay. But I loved Versailles and I was determined to spend the time, insofar as my circumstances and the proper forms for a lady visitor permitted, on my own. I was of course adept at making myself scarce, in heart and mind at least, when others were fussing around. My first visits with my aunt to the palace had taught me how. But this time felt different. It was the most glorious opportunity – I had been living in his apartment for several months by then – for me to be at last, if only this one time, all by myself. In any case, should a different urge overtake me, Versailles was rich in possibilities. The chauffeur pretended to make for Vatel's, it was lunch by the time we arrived, while I used the brief moment of his absence – he would make the circuit and head right back to find me within minutes – to lose myself in the crowds of the Diana drawing room.

While the people in the room raised their heads to the gold-encrusted ceiling, where Diana was painted in her chariot presiding over the hunt and the seas, I turned to my favourite painting above the chimney place. There she was again, quiver on her back, arm outstretched to Agamemnon, whose knife has dropped from his hand. While Iphegenia, one breast naked, dishevelled hair drooping down her back, looks lovingly up to her protectress with a mixture of astonishment and relief. The worst can befall and not befall you. Did a parent betray

165

you? They can do you no damage. If you believe hard enough, you will be saved in the nick of time. You have been robbed. Steal the day from under you. Steal away.

Armed with my guidebook, I headed for the Queen's bedchamber, last occupied – before she fled the Revolution – by Marie Antoinette. A room where I like to stand and think, a room so gallooned with gold it almost hurts the eyes, golden sculptures swelling from the corners of the ceiling, gilt on all the wainscoting, gold threads edging the wall hangings, gold-embroidered lampas fabric, gold on the railings of the balustrade which grants and forbids access to the Queen's bed. When she wished to retire – when all the royals retired – either she or her retainer had first to open a gate. No one passed straight into the Queen's intimacy, no one slipped easily into her dark, not even the Queen herself.

In the corners sculptures of naked women stretch out their golden bodies as if the whole room relied on their exertion to hold the cornice in place. Above the Queen's bed, on either side of the canopy, clusters of ostrich feathers loop over the ends, a little nod, as I see them, to the most hidden parts of her body – not that, while we all stand there, anyone is supposed to be considering such things – concealed beneath the heavily embroidered covers of her bed. As she looked up, she could see the white tufts, the only thing in the room that moves, or sitting square between them, Boucher's painting of *The Queen's Virtues*, she could rise above or, as I like to think, gently comb her own niche. Although even *The Queen's Virtues* does not seem to depict quite what you would expect. Danaë's head is thrown back, her eyes are to the heavens, she is swathed in the densest fabric, but with one naked foot pointing out from beneath her skirts, and lying across the bottom of the painting is a naked cherub, his belly plump, arms behind his head clutching bundles of grapes, which appear to be falling out of his hair. In the gardens the fountain for autumn was Bacchus wreathed and fairly spilling with grapes, looking not as he should on to the next season of winter, but, leery-eyed and flouting the symmetry of the gardens, in the direction of summer. At Ceres surrounded by naked cupids and offerings of wild flowers, blissfully watching the stream of water shooting up towards the foliage above her head. Was the Queen's virtue then to lower her eyes? Alone in her bedchamber – there must have been such times – what exactly was she meant to be looking at?

By now the room was stifling, so I made my way down the Queen's marble staircase and out through the courtyard to the gardens. I knew I was being followed, but thought it wiser not to let my pursuer know that I knew. That way he would keep at it without suspecting for a second that he had become part of my plan instead of the other way round. I would run the risk that it was not him on my heels but something rather more dangerous and promising as a price worth paying for his ignorance. There was a world between him following me at the behest of his master, and him doing exactly the same thing, unbeknown to the two of them, as I willed. He was looking for a scandal. He had, I was certain, been primed. But nothing seemed so perfectly scandalous to me as him snooping after me among the crowds blind to my foresight. Were they then dazed by my innocence? And by nothing so much? For my friend at home, this was, I am sure, my worst offence. The very idea would have ripped the ground from beneath his feet. I could picture him sitting comfortably reassured at home, full of self-congratulation,

167

underestimating me – how he underestimated me! – yet again. So, I decided, I would string them along, keep him in mind only enough to keep myself at liberty, and then forget about them both. Of course I know that real freedom is not wilful, assertive or clever, even then as I thought myself. Real freedom, the one I am inching towards slowly but surely, will be when I soar – I will be soaring – and he dwindles to nothing, a tiny vanishing speck on a horizon I can no longer even see.

I swept down the central concourse into the gardens along the water parterre, its two pools designed with exact precision to reflect the façade of the palace behind them, whose lines plunge headlong into the water. As if a building, in defiance of all the weight above ground, could go thirsting after its own roots. In Versailles there is water everywhere. Not just hidden in the marshes, sapping at gravity, but everywhere to see. Water in the fountains that greet you at every turn, water in the pools, water of the King's mirror pond, water of the rock-work grove, avenue of water, water of the Grand Canal, which stretches its arms to the four points of the compass. Its engineer had dreamt of making a link from Versailles to the Loire and from there to the Mediterranean and Atlantic ports of France. So great was the need for water in his gardens that Louis XIV even attempted to deviate the river Eure from its course. The challenge presented to his magnificence by water, the difficulty of bridling the elements, was far greater than any problems the King confronted in the collecting, hoarding and crafting of diamonds and pearls and gold. If you want to be seen to be rich, you will encrust yourself. At the risk of then finding that you are weighed down by your own splendour, that you have made yourself, however grandly you are guarded, a mere toything, the too-easy prey for thieves and traitors and saboteurs. But if you want to be a god and possess more than the wealth of nations, you will send the waters swirling, bubbling and spouting over every available surface of the earth.

As I drifted along, I felt I was gliding on a sheet of water. Glances were thrown in my direction, eyes focused on me for a second and then just as quickly moved past. It was not customary for a young woman to walk unaccompanied through the gardens, but whether that fact should make me conspicuous or invisible was, I think to everyone, unclear. To cover both options, my anonymous companions of the walkways stared and then stared away. As I made my way boldly up and down the avenues, I would occasionally incline my head. I didn't recognise a soul. But I live in a world where everyone goes so in dread of a *faux pas* that only someone deliberately making one at every turn could be so delightfully sure of herself. One by one, without fail, they returned my gesture, held it for a moment and then let it float off like a bubble. In the perfect understanding that the last thing they were meant to do was stop. I was dressed in a black satin dress, white bodice for relief – it was after all late summer – with white lace gloves, and carrying a white and black striped parasol. I must have looked like someone emerging from a long period of mourning who has just granted themselves the first hint of a reprieve. My elegance gave me ground. I proceeded on my path with the confidence of a countess whose train of valets and attendants, without her having even noticed, is loitering around the last corner, three steps behind her in the park.

When I turned away towards the sides of the gardens, I glimpsed the chauffeur at the top end of the east–west avenue, shading his eyes as he peered down in search of me past the Latona fountain, along the Royal Avenue to the fountain of Apollo, the path which you are meant to take if you are following the perspective of the King. When he looked out of his window, he liked his gaze to fall upon Apollo riding his chariot and steeds, which buck and rear out of the water straight under the midday point of the sun. If you are proceeding along the indicated path, you have to walk past Latona to reach Apollo. Two spirits cut from the same cloth. Scourge of proud mortals, he was truly his mother's son. She presides over her company of frogs, peasants until they scorned her and she brought the wrath of Jupiter down on their backs. In and out of her water they leap, condemned to remain in the orbit of her curse. Cautionary tales. Versailles is full of them. You can choose, though. You can always pick and choose.

I turned north by north-west towards the fountain of the rebel giant Enceladus, a gnarled mass of bronze, almost blinding in the mid-afternoon sun. Not perhaps, most obviously, comfort to the restless. He is almost buried under rocks, the heavy, bitter fruits of his own revolt, which came crashing down on him when he cast them to the heavens in defiance of Jupiter and the gods. A lattice enclosure has been built all around him, so he is the only figure in the gardens who looks like someone trapped in a cage. The only one allowed to suffer, carrying the burden, as I see it, for so many of the rest. After all, you have to get people to admit you are suffering before you can even begin to protest. Almost the whole of his torso is covered by the stones, large lumps of granite like bits of brain which seem to have been carved out of the inside of his huge, muscular head. But there he lies undefeated, a rock still in his hand, mouth open to hurl his jet of water – one last curse – at the skies. A body more monumental and powerful than any you will see in Versailles.

It was a few moments before I realised my pursuer had caught up with me. A few more before I realised it wasn't me he was watching. He was gawping at Enceladus. This, I should stress, is not so strange or as unlikely as it might at first seem. There are beautiful bodies all over Versailles, Greek gods and goddesses of divinely modulated proportions everywhere. Like nothing on earth. Of course. Whereas, because the magnificence of Enceladus's body is desperate and hopeless, it is at least conceivable that, whatever his strength, he just might be in need of something, or even somebody, else. I had my own reasons for admiring a sculpture of someone not quite drowning in his own rage. But that, I understood, was not exactly the point. Unlike the other statues in the gardens, Enceladus was vexed and encumbered, but he was also boundless. It made him inviting. Certainly, despite the superficial similarities of ligament and curve, he wasn't at all like Octave, who seemed to ask nothing more of his body than that it would silently and unostentatiously deflate. Octave wanted to be adored but not touched. Whereas every muscle in the body of Enceladus bore monumental witness to a rather different proposition. That adoration is strictly for the gods.

I had been staring at the statue for a while. I turned just in time to see my chauffeur, together with an unidentified male companion, disappearing into the trees. And into who knows what outer precincts of the grounds beyond. As one of my guidebooks once put it, the central park of Versailles is ordered for France, while the acres all around – to symbolise the rest of the world – are wild.

A calm and joy washed over me. When the two of

171

them disappeared, they took the heat of the day and all cruelty – of my and their predicament – with them. Press a weight down hard on somebody's chest and then lift it. After the first shock they will breathe more freely and greedily, relishing the air that saves them, than ever before. It was two o'clock in the afternoon. Whichever way you turned, parasols were raised against the glare. But to me even the sun felt cool. And the whole place, crowded from end to end as it always was at this time of the year, deserted.

I stood there for a while. I had to hold steady. It felt as though I was suspended in my own little pool of air and light and if I moved I would start floating. All my props had gone. Everything I hated most, fought hardest against, just dropped away. I thought I would fall. I had my own favourite path through Versailles. But, for it to work, for me to make the most of it, I needed the presence of someone or other I was trying to leave behind. Someone who, even if I managed to fox them, would remain loyally inside my head for me to fume against. You see, I can get away from you. You, you, you. But if they turn away? Or, worse, if no one is there? By the mere uncalculated act of removing himself with another, letting me drop from his mind for the sake of his own enjoyment, the chauffeur had taught me a lesson. Although not quite the one that either of them, chauffeur or master, had planned. I could feel the currents shift. As if tiny slivers of metal, at random till that moment, had been sucked on to the ends of a magnet suddenly appearing in their midst. Captive in his home I may have been, but I had been as possessive as he was all along. Never for a second had I even entertained the possibility that he took pleasure in anyone but me. It was all right for me to be one of three, or four or even more.

But not him. With a dawning recognition that turned me sick to the stomach, I realised. The more he trapped me, the better. It was the only way I could be sure that I was the one he was looking at. It was the only guarantee.

Now my pursuer had taken off on his own cloud and the whole world was fading away. All the trees around me seemed to be groaning at their new-found lightness. And the anger I had come daily to rely on was left floundering, bereft. Pain stood back. Insulted to be so summarily dismissed. I was completely at a loss. For the first time in my life, I had absolutely no idea what to do next. Light-headed as I felt, I didn't think I would faint – I have never fainted. I was not disappearing. I was being brought up closer. Whatever was about to happen, I was not going to be allowed to get away from myself.

Slowly, afraid that if I moved too fast everyone would know what was happening, I gathered myself together, opened up my parasol in deference to the season and moved on. I was quite convinced that my inner state was written over my face for everyone to see. Since they could not possibly understand, I assumed as they stood aside almost hushed to let me past, that I must look like someone overwhelmed by an unexpected, suddenly recurring grief. Someone who had been let out – how right they were! – a little too soon. They avoided me like someone contagious, but as if nothing would be worse than to let anybody else know I was carrying a fatal disease because of the panic it would send hurtling across the grounds. Striking down all composure, pressing bodies, as they hurried in all directions, dangerously against each other in the rush. Never have I felt so conspicuous, so exposed – humiliated almost – as at that moment. The one time when at last I found myself isolated, alone on the little island of my own which I had been longing for most of my life.

Hesitantly I picked my way through my own debris across the park, shedding and amassing the pieces like a night warden collecting leaves in the dusk. I wanted to get to the Grand Trianon. I thought if I moved under its arches, allowed myself the vistas which open out from its gardens, I would be able to retrieve myself. I wanted to repeat something, although I was not altogether sure what it was or why. I walked along, head held high and steady, but I felt as if I was scrambling in the dust. Once you leave the main concourse of the gardens, sand lines the walkways. One pace ahead of me, it seemed to be stirring, tiny specks of yellow banking my pathway with clouds. I turned the corner on to the grand alley that leads up the hill on top of which sits the Trianon, higher off the ground than the castle. There in front of me I could see the colonnade, arch after arch, with nothing – when you are down below – but bright patches of sky in between. I walked through the gate and started circling the arches, lightly touching, skirts brushing, each pillar as I passed. Violet and slate-blue, they seemed to have drenched their surface in the deepest colours of the sky.

I drifted into the building, where I had been so many times before, and stood, for what seemed like an age, in front of the huge desk and chair in the cabinet of the Emperor, his privileged and chosen place of work. The place where he went to read and write and think. I had never really looked at it before. The chair stared back at me. A massive, forbidding dark-wood construct, the whole apparently sculpted in one swathe from a single piece of wood, with its back to the light, laid its shadow over the desk where he worked. And then I noticed, carved away right in the middle of its vast expanse, small thin arches, openings which would have let straight into the hollow of his back as he sat there tiny, stubborn, pockets of light. Only the smallest hand could have crafted spaces so fine, like the first vertical threads of netting before it is spun into filigree. You could be Emperor or King and retreat from the world to your mind. A world which waits on your summons. But behind you, in a place no one can ever see once you are seated, you too might want nothing so much as to feel the slow sweet pressure of the air.

I left the room as one delivered from a dreadful sentence. Standing in front of Enceladus I had allowed myself to imagine that he had put me out of his mind and I was gasping. It had been like a stab to the back of the throat. But now the world was rotating. He was suffocating as much as I was. Where does he go, where did the Emperor go, when seated at his desk, pen in hand, writing to save the state and nation, struggling to grasp at his own legacy before he died, he felt the light filtering invisibly into his body and the warmth make its way into his bones through the back of his chair?

Normally when I left the Grand Trianon I would have turned left along the path to the Queen's garden of the Petit Trianon. I would have sat under the huge, split formation of rocks which open to the sky, covering you, if occasion requires it, from prying eyes. And on from there to the rustic hamlet of Marie Antoinette. It had always struck me as a poor but tragic joke at her expense that she could be allowed her little place in the country on condition that she never left the palace grounds. But on that day I was looking for clues. I hailed a horse carriage – my confidence and my resolve were flooding back – and directed it to return me to the central concourse. Once there we headed south-west from Apollo to the mirror pond, behind which, half hidden, I knew there was a garden for the King.

You can walk around this garden several times before you find the entry. You can wander up and down the diagonal paths which frame it on every side, skirting the hedgerows and marvelling at the curious trees that weave in and out, occasionally rising and offering their strange-shaped foliage above the bushes. You have never seen these trees before. In the Queen's garden of the Petit Trianon, you meet a feast of names and places – almond and peach, white walnut and black beech, pine from Lord Weymouth, Japanese pagoda, silver maple from America, Canadian fir, aspen and silk-cotton tree. You are being instructed to find your royal bearings, not just in the garden, but in every furthest reach of the globe. But for the King's garden there is nothing. When you finally turn through the small opening in the hedgerow, a vast oval lawn stretches out before you. So difficult is this garden of access, so tucked away from the rest of Versailles, so hedged and protected, you wrongly imagine that, like the most closely guarded and intimate of personal treasures, it will be minuscule.

There in the centre, two huge isolated plane trees – the only ones I could name – uncluttered by order or undergrowth surge upwards into the air. All around the central stretch of green are little open coves of grass, miniature lawns like antechambers to the private rooms of the King. In Versailles the flowers are always tended and perfect, but here they are planted in patterned mounds carved out of the lawn, not so as to reflect back on to the majesty of the buildings, but shedding their radiance on to

176

the grass. And on each side are the hedges you passed along, back and forwards, before you were graced with entry, out of which trees of uneven heights and different colours and shapes rise up without competing with the planes on the central lawn. Nothing matches, but nothing jars. This is the harmony of disproportion. Branches twisting, vines clinging to bark, trees bending over bushes, all of it allowed to germinate freely without collapsing into the wild. A true hall of mirrors – unlike the hateful one in the palace – in this garden everything reflects something other than itself.

At the centre of the main lawn, there is one solitary white tower, almost thrown by its own loftiness, on which nothing seems to rely. Nothing hangs on this. And if on either side at each of the far ends of the gardens there are indeed, predictably enough, two white statues, they appear to carry no message. For once in all this great domain, it doesn't seem to matter, not even to them, who – whether in or out of this world – they are. My chauffeur, for all I cared, could well have gathered himself together and come after me. But even if he was standing there at that moment he wouldn't intrude. Nobody would find me here, not in a way which concerned me, because nothing in this garden had the faintest interest in being recognised or found. In fact I was at last ready to return to the city. All I had needed was to discover a place where I could, just once, imagine him free of himself. No threat, all power gone. I could get up and walk away without a trace of fear. Take your time, I was telling myself. Now you can really leave. I made my way out of the King's garden past the mirror pool just as it was catching the rays of the sinking sun. And then up the grand avenue through the garden grille to the front courtyard of the palace, where the chauffeur, as if invisibly summoned, sat waiting for me in his motorcar. When he handed me into my seat I was overcome with a wondrous sense of achievement. I had spent seven hours, not one minute wasted, in the palace and gardens of Versailles.

—

When I returned to the city I felt held in a mist, wrapped inside one of those moist clouds which hover over the lake at Versailles. Why hurry? you can almost hear them saying as they drift and float one way and another making scarcely an imprint on the deep deep blue of the sky. Why shed the rain? I had finished with him. Of that I was now certain, and for a while at least it was enough for me to know. Octave and Andrée and Esther could be relied on to do the rest. But he was not finished with me, and in the week that followed I could feel him trying to seize my day at the palace and twist it back and forwards in his mind, squeezing the life out of it, like a servant wringing a floorcloth before slapping it on to the flagstones, or snapping off the head of a chicken who, for minutes after the deed has been done, carries on racing around. He would do everything he could to tarnish my time, even though the day was gone. Why couldn't he see that it was his own freedom, far more than mine, which he was crumpling in his fist and hurling straight back into the fire?

Exactly a week later, when I was still bathing in my own solace, he marched into my room and suggested we went for a drive. 'Versailles,' he said. Where else? I was sitting dressed in one of his finest gifts, a Fortuny dressing gown, one of the several Fortuny gowns he had procured for me because Venice inspired him, and because it suited him to think of me as someone of royal or noble distinction and freedom, a doge's lady gracing and making her way in public spaces. Provided that, as soon as he had built the picture, he could thrust it safely away into history, frame it with a golden hue which increasingly he could only imagine – although modern-day versions were everywhere all around us – in distant, long-lost times. More and more he liked to embellish me. No more lightness. No more frippery. He was driving back the sea, which was rapidly disappearing even as memory. I sat there in state, in wreaths of thick silk falling in pleats all over me, the deepest sapphire which at each lift of my arm, the tiniest movement of my legs or feet, glinted and miraculously transformed into liquid bronze. Deep pink lined the inside of my sleeves as if a profusion of flowers, clamped away against nature, in protest had run their colours fast into each other and stained the insides of the earth. And all over the body of the gown, almost invisible to the wearer, were tiny images of birds. The last sign I was to be allowed that there was anything anywhere existing in the world which truly had the freedom of the skies.

He was deadly serious. He had of course been interrogating the chauffeur but, given what I'd seen, I knew I could rest easy on that score. But if I was not to arouse my friend's suspicions, I had to move fast. There had to be not one breath of hesitation. For in the flash of such a moment, I knew a chasm would open up between us into which our shared delusion – his determined belief that we were still in this together – would instantly and irrevocably fall. 'Versailles. Of course. I'd love to. And it's a perfect day. If we don't get out of the car, there is no need for me to change. I can just pull a coat over my dressing gown.' I walked over to where my coats were hanging and pushed two or three of them aside one after the other, head to one side, studying and thinking, so as to convince him that selecting the right one was my only care. As if my rush to please were not a giveaway, as if such naked obedience were not truly indecent.

So he put me through my paces, shunted us around the palace and gardens, against his own frailty, for what seemed an interminable time. Within minutes of our arrival, perhaps even before we set out, he had obviously decided that I was heavily covered enough, that modesty, one way and another, not being the issue, there was no need for us to remain in the motorcar. Although he did not leave my side for a second, I felt as if I was being followed, so studied was his accompaniment, so earnestly was he trying to work out, copy, replicate in minutest detail my earlier tune. He was like a lover who in madness feels his jealousy will only be assuaged if his mistress not only admits that she has another lover, but tells him, even rehearses for his most perverse pleasure, each trick she performs in the other's arms. At every turn he cast me sidelong glances. In fact I do not think he ever, even when appearing to look ahead, quite took his eyes off me. To the world we were a couple, side by side, enjoying the clear skies and warmth of a late summer's day. But I have never felt less like his equal, and never – although I was as good as walking on his arm – less communion between his body and mine. A trick of the light. A happy duo gliding in perfect harmony. But look again and see what happens when, noticing there are not one but two filters inside the lantern, you start to prise them apart. He is pacing her, she his quarry, or even – something I never believed he wanted – a few steps behind, eyes lowered to the ground, the dutiful, bowing, fawning, concubine.

And all the while we walked the grounds, my anguish increased by the minute, not for myself – with every step I added stroke upon stroke to my new life – but for him. Cramped, doubled over on himself, with me as mere pretext, exhausted, shunting back and forth along the narrow straits of his mind. Versailles was glinting, even brighter today than before, but its brightness was no reproach to me. The whole place, my silent witness. Appalled, perhaps, by what I seemed to have been reduced to, but still filled with my mood of just a week ago, charging me up with my own memory. Inside my coat I could feel my dressing gown swish against my knees, its pleats clinging to my thighs, sweeping the air up my legs, up and up, from the ground.

On the drive back, we stopped at a famous pâtisserie a mile north of the town. Coming out clutching her parcels, the governess whom I had seen playing cards with her mistress at Mlle Léa's swept through the door and, forcing us to stand aside, down the steps. Her face was flushed and guilty, as if even this most simple and innocent of domestic outings carried the aura of her secret life. For the space of a second she caught my eye. Just a flicker of recognition. At the house of Mlle Léa, not a murmur had passed between us. I didn't even think she had noticed me. But today our new setting – the afternoon glare, his presence – made us companions of that other domain. She put up her free hand to the bright orange feathered hat which looped down over one side of her face and straightened the veil. I raised mine to the back of my head and loosening the pin as if my hat were about to slip, took it out and then immediately fastened it back into exactly the same place. Nothing escaped him. It had turned into an uncomfortably humid afternoon. To the unobservant at least, we were two women coiffed and composed. But in that fleeting gesture with which we adjusted our already perfectly adjusted garments, we had managed, like a couple of careless streetwalkers, to make ourselves louche and undressed. The smell of pastry, rising yeast, baked honey, melted butter, burnt sugar wafted out of the partly open door. Cloaked in the aromas, grateful for their cover, I preceded him up the steps and into the shop, where we sat down together for tea.

This was new. We had, I suddenly realised, never been in conflict before out of doors. I had never had to register anger written all over a face which, with the yellow light streaming through the windows on to the chequered-cloth tables, I could so clearly and shockingly see. No shade, no thick curtains, no heavy indoor garments or blankets packing him away to his own corners, as he sat curled up huddling on his sofa or bed. Nor a face holding itself so close that – robbing you of the familiarity it seems so boldly to offer, instantly unrecognisable – pieces slide from the centre and all proportions capsize. True ugliness comes in between. He was illuminated in the cold light of his own stare. I could see every mark and pore and vein, every smallest shift in the tone of his flesh as his colour – he never had much colour – pushed itself forward and pulled back from the surface of his skin. His dilemma was chalked all over his countenance. You could feel the blood rise and baulk, joining in his hesitation, one step ahead of his whim. As if the insides of his body knew before he did that this time, the moment he started talking, the one he would be giving away, nakedly, once and for all, was himself.

Like a kidnap victim in one of the melodramas of the boulevards, sitting with her captors, a gun pointing at her under the table which only the audience can see, I had been shooting plaintive, meaningful glances at the proprietress. A bit of a comedy if what was being asked was that she save my life or my virtue since, in relation to the second, our lady of the teacakes, bursting with her own generosity, was renowned. Imploringly I gazed up at her as she bustled around clearing and setting the tables, even though her tearoom was steadily emptying in the late afternoon. But insensible to everything apart from the delicious savour of her own tasks, she wouldn't even catch my eye. Her perfect, studied indifference gave him his cue. He started, his voice barely above a whisper. On to the table he poured his accusations like a small boy retching without relief. He knew far more than I had thought and far less than he believed. It was irrelevant, since it was so obviously his confession, not mine.

Avoiding his eyes, I let mine fall, while still keeping track of my proprietress, whose ability to cut herself off from unwelcome entreaty now seemed not rude, not cruel, but wise. With one hand in my lap, I closed my coat tight over my skirts shoving back any stray pleats of my gown. And then sat there stirring my tea long after the sugar had dissolved, listening to the faint ringing tone sound and fade each time the tiny gold spoon, as it went round and round and round, grazed the porcelain.

At this time of year Paris is caught between two seasons. The heat is starting to lift, citizens are returning, streets are filling with sound after the August hush. Light-headed, the city only just holds steady, drunk on the vacuum of a summer almost past, drunk on the promise of plenty to come. Along the Boulevard Haussmann the financiers and traders are not yet treading the pavement, there is just the hum of the tramway, sometimes a horse-drawn carriage and – heralded by fumes which seep through all defences – the occasional motorcar. In the quiet the horses' hooves striking the flagstones could almost be mistaken for the clip of a farmer's shire horse on a country lane. Paris is waiting. Excited but awkward, like a society gentleman, the subject of gossip which has not yet reached him, who – eager, a little nervous – has sent out all his visiting cards. It is the only point in the year when the city seems unsure of itself.

Back in my room, I take comfort from these broken bits of silence. They tell me that Paris has not abandoned her daughters, that she will eventually return to her normal shape. Although, when I get up and walk towards the windows, I feel as if I am the mother who, after months, even years, of dreadful foreboding is preparing – ecstatic but with a calm she could never have predicted – to greet her runaway child. The handle of the windows has gone stiff with disuse. I have almost to force it before it gives, rattling it up and down, muffling the sound with my fist, and then angrily letting go. In all weathers, a wall of heat radiates from his apartment. Damp has been dripping inside the window frame where the warmth meets the air of the street. Once the windows part, folding back to the wall, splinters of wood break off and drop. The thick brocade curtains are smothered behind the glass, like the skirts of anxious debutantes crushed into an alcove. Before stepping on to the balcony, I pull them free so they hang in the open light, blocking the world behind. If anyone walks in, they will, at least for a moment, have no idea where I am. They just might think a thief, after sprinting improbably up the surface of the building, is now, his fingers clasped to the railings, holding on to the balcony for dear life. A cloud of tiny grey particles, the dust which has been gathering for years in the folds of the curtains, drifts off into the day. As I stand before them, poised against their golden backdrop above the city, I hear them swish behind me, laying stroke upon stroke over the dark. Numb from pulling, my fingers take a while to feel the breeze which creeps up my arms until – with a blast so decisive it could be midwinter – it stuns the world back into my cheeks.

For several days now, my floor has been covered with boxes not yet filled. I haven't quite decided how much of me to take with me when I go. As soon as I asked for them, almost before I turned away, and without so much as blinking, Adèle had them brought to my room. She has been praying for this moment from the day I arrived. Fearful of wrecking my plans, she will not tell him. So I can take as long as I choose. And I have sent Andrée the note which, since our visit to Mlle Léa, I know she has been expecting by the hour. 'No hurry, whichever day suits you, so long as it is before the dawn. Bring Octave in his motorcar.' I will have my cortège. Now it is only a matter of time.

PART FOUR

I DID it for Albertine, agreeing to visit him in October, when nearly all the birds had gone from the parks and only the pigeons remained, staining the buildings grey to match the weather. More than a month had passed since we had left her in the country, Octave, Esther and I, but only a few weeks or even days, to judge from his hastily scrawled note, since her trail had gone cold. Suddenly there had been no more communication, so she had, I assumed, simply stopped bothering. For a while he couldn't hear her silence, but now, true to form, he wanted to turn it into an opportunity, another chance to command. 'Dear Andrée, please come quickly. Something is wrong.' He would panic me into coming, since he never stopped believing that everyone who had ever come near her needed as much as he did to know what was happening to Albertine.

On my way through the city I told myself it was what she would have wanted. So it was business as usual, I suppose, both of us leaping to her attention, with somebody serving and somebody being served. Only as I turned the corner of the Boulevard Malesherbes, retracing backwards the steps of our afternoon walks to the park, did I start to wonder why on earth I was going. To be one of his party was the last thing I desired. Gradually, uneasily, I had been making my peace with her. No one had been as close as I, together the three of us had plucked her from his path, and yet she had managed to wipe out the distance between us and him. One more masterstroke on her part, and there we were, reluctant partners, not to say bedfellows, each and every one. After all, she had dropped the whole lot of us more or less at exactly the same time.

Octave was the one to broach the matter. 'Don't you feel,' he said one afternoon as we sat together taking tea by the Opéra – we had been studiously avoiding any mention of Albertine – 'don't you feel a bit put upon?' He was looking straight at me. Esther, dreamily staring into the middle distance, might as well not have been there. We both knew she had only ever really been borrowed and would pull out at any time she chose since, her passion for Mlle Léa notwithstanding, she never saw herself as stopping anywhere. 'Don't be silly,' she swung her gaze round towards us. 'People come and go.' But Octave had a grievance. For Albertine's sake, he had slowed down and, now at a complete standstill, he feared that at any moment he might fall flat on his face. With a tinge of irritation, he insisted. 'Well, don't you?' I said nothing. I didn't want his wounded allegiance. Even in misery, I wasn't going to share her.

Visiting him was quite another matter since I could tell myself that he was bound to be ridiculous and that whatever I found myself saying, with every anxious query on his part, the gulf would yawn a little bit wider between her and him. I would be rescuing her all over again.

At the familiar sound of the latch clicking, I pushed

open the heavy door from the street. The day was past its peak, no light fell into the inner courtyard, and even before I crossed over to the stairs the place seemed empty. Since I had never set foot in his apartment without her being there, I started to feel like a nasty little usurper betraying her best friend. He appeared at the door of his room in moccasin slippers and a heavy dressing gown woven in small black and white squares, which made him look oddly like a chequer board, something an invalid, worried to be summoning people in his condition, might offer for the entertainment of his guests. It was five o'clock in the afternoon. 'You poor man.' Suddenly sad and overcome on his behalf, I lowered my eyes. He looked positively gratified.

In the past our contact had always followed the same pattern. I told him what he wanted to hear, that she and I were inseparable, which was of course true. I never lied. What for? He wanted me to watch over her and so I did, just a touch more, let's say, than he surmised, although the allegiance between him and me was real enough, even if I had never seen it till then. Each of us was happy to build our lives around her, so long as she was the one wanting. She mustn't be unhappy as that would have spoiled things, rocked the boat too far, but just needy enough, dependent enough to make us feel indispensable. We were her joint protectors, the parents she had never had, and we were meeting today like a long-separated couple brought together by the death of a child.

We walked into a drawing room which, clouded from the light like the rest of his apartment, looked as if it had hardly ever been used. 'I am so sorry to be in such a rush, but I'm having dinner with Gisèle and I promised to drop round before we go out. I really can only stop for a short while.' Although the haste with which I had taken off my coat, my gloves, my muff, my hat, must have given quite the wrong impression, of someone overjoyed to be there who cannot wait to be settled in.

With a strange sense of foreboding, I sank down, almost disappearing, into one of his plush drawing-room chairs. The room felt slanted and he definitely wasn't in the right place. From everything she had told me, I knew he hated to be the one standing. He was taller than I had thought. I took a deep breath, not easy in such airless surroundings, and prepared myself to tell him what was after all the truth – that I no longer had any idea where she was. 'I hardly thought you would.' He drew up a chair close beside me so our legs were almost touching and leant across till he was facing my eyes. In the past he had always been casual, putting his requests lightly, as though what he was asking was the natural concern of a friend and of course to the advantage of Albertine. Our whole charade had been enormously helped by the fact that, three times out of four, he chose to reach me by means of the telephone, so he could rehearse the voice behind a face which I realised, as we now blinked awkwardly at each other, I had never really bothered to look at before. His skin was flawless, his eyes so round he must always look like someone who had either just received shocking news or was struggling to get a delicate question into words. His thick black, slightly wavy, hair was exactly the same colour as hers. I resisted the temptation to lean over and stroke it. 'But you do know her, dear Andrée, far better than I.' A fire in the grate caught the light of his eye, and the whole room, quivering from the flicker of the flames, shone in its polished ball. How on earth, Albertine, how on earth did you survive? I reasoned with her silently, but I would never have dreamt of asking her any such thing had she been there.

He took my hand and held it between his as though he was about to tell me something which would be very difficult for me to hear. On the other hand, since I was the one who was meant to do the talking, he reminded me of a father confessor making a special effort to be kind so as to conceal his rising excitement at the prospect of listening to a young girl's litany of sin. I had always wondered why the holy fathers of the Church could not see the wonderful trap they sprang on their own purity, how completely they exposed themselves when they leant forward inside their dark hovel – you can always hear the rustle of the robes – as if to say, 'You can tell me. I already know.' My first response, since I was under no obligation to him to say anything any more, came out almost unthinking, 'How can you even imagine such a thing?' For a moment we both took comfort from the neatness of this solution, with its tidy little script: he had lost his love, I my dearest friend, and we were the companions of a tragedy, which must, of course, bring us closer. With a mournful sigh, he squeezed my hand, upon which I blurted out, 'Well, maybe me, yes me. But Albertine never, she never knew anything about that side of my life and had no such tastes at all.' I felt like a piece of livebait who had wriggled free from a wire, but before I had barely had time to relax, I could see Albertine, face at the window, hammering at the pane. 'How could you? How could you leave me out in the cold? Say anything, let him think, if it will help that, whatever pleasures you and I took, he was the one who I wanted to rescue me and turn the world to rights. Then neither of you, quite, lose me. But *tell him*.'

He didn't release his hold, but, leaning over, ran his free

193

hand down the side of my face. 'Nothing you could say will surprise me, nothing that the two of you – of course, dearest Andrée, I know it must have been the two of you – could do. Such delights are not repugnant to me. Far from it, it gives me the greatest pleasure to think of you so together. Why don't you return after your dinner with Gisèle, and show me what you girls are capable of? Nor is there any need for you to feel awkward. I shall – how shall I put it? – be watching you in one way, while in another I will not be looking at the two of you at all. You will allow me to think about her, about her happiest moments which I now realise, perhaps indeed I knew it all along, it was with you that she enjoyed.'

'Of course my greatest aim was to allow her whatever pleased her.' He was magnificent and, inspired by his own eloquence, he got to his feet at last, letting go of my hand. For a moment I thought he was going to take a bow. I was furious, but I was not going to let him see, since to flare up this close would have felt like throwing myself at his feet. As though on cue, Adèle walked into the room carrying a tea tray with a silver tea set, white and gold cups and saucers, and a plate of petits fours and brioches which I recognised as being from Rabattet and Chez Bourbon-neux. She placed it down on a brown marbled table which so blended with the obscurity that, until that moment, I had mistaken it for a fur cape on a chair, and stood waiting with her arms folded in silence, although it was easy enough for me to read her mind – 'Don't think, my little hussy, that with her gone, it's your turn next. Over my dead body.' 'Or,' I thought to myself, since whatever had happened to Albertine, he was surely the real casualty of the whole sorry affair, 'his.' Having made her point,

194

she turned away and left the room as abruptly as she had arrived.

'If that's what you want,' I said to him in my mind, 'you can have it.' I wasn't going to show him or perform for him, since, whether we liked it or not, he had been the invisible witness of Albertine's and my silent communion for too long. But I would tell him and tell him and never stop telling him until he got the point which she had only been able – was still trying? – to make with her escape. You can listen. Perhaps one day somebody, not today and not me, will let you see, but however you twist and turn, cajole and bribe, this is something you cannot do. This is somewhere no man can ever be.

Saying that – and I said more and more and more – I still found myself wondering whether my victory was over him or, as I finally gave our game away, over her. For even if it is what she would have wanted, even if while I spoke I felt her voice migrate from its plaint at the window into mine, never in all the time I had known her had I ever pretended to speak on behalf of Albertine.

'So that is why she left me?' It was a question, but the tone of his voice brooked no argument. He had sat down again, like an army general who has just won a crucial battle eyeing the devastation which his own genius has wreaked. His arms lay on the rests of his chair and his legs were stretched out almost horizontally over the carpet in front of him so his whole body seemed to point like a shaft of ice in one stiff angle at the floor. He was chilled by his own declaration, shocked by the force with which he had wrested a truth even if he was convinced it was one he had always known, and even if it left him more puzzled than before. With his head bent, he stared at the relic of his own bittersweet anticipation. 'You fool.' I leapt to my feet and rushed over to him, tears running down my cheeks. 'You fool. Don't you see? You should have married her!' He took my hand again and, this time with a mildness which surprised us both, he drew me down towards him, making his claim on her for one last time. She was all over us, shining so hard and bright you would think that she had swallowed the sun.

At my aunt's villa, you can reach the river from the bottom of the garden. There is a longer way round through the village, but if you don't mind pushing past the bushes and stepping over the taller grass where the gardener's labours abruptly cease, you arrive at an old gate, its paint peeling, its hinges gone to rust. Half-open, bent, it is raised slightly skew to the ground, like someone caught and then frozen with their arm in the air. Clutching my skirts, hems lifted, I can just squeeze past and out on to the field which runs headlong down to the bank.

At the bottom of the field a cluster of trees, their tapering branches skimming the surface of the water, almost hides the river from view. Even if someone had been watching me run down through the field, they would not be able to see me take off my robe to bathe in the earliest hours of the morning, when the quietness, so full you can almost hear it, is the only thing that might alert the sleeping in their beds. Heads lifted, bodies which fret and turn, their tiny particles of skin and moisture flaking and sinking through the covers, before all thought, aroused for the merest second, seeps back into the pillows again. It is now late September. The finest haze hovers over the water like a thin film of dust which has floated up from a polished surface and then stayed. When I step into the river, the haze, the water, and the lean rays of the morning sun, fold over, thickening into each other, to cover my neck, my arms and throat. I want no followers, no attendants, never again anyone ever to watch over me. But as I trail the water behind me, I allow myself just for a while to imagine the whole world, latched to my every movement, turning itself into my retinue.

I have been coming here every day since I arrived just over a month ago. Those who served me — Octave, Esther, Andrée — rushing to my summons almost before it was even spoken, simply deposited me at the villa and departed, taking their fears — from which they considered themselves to have saved me — with them as they went. Perhaps they would have done better to leave them here in my keeping so they could dissolve and melt away in the sun as it slowly builds up throughout the morning and begins to encircle and warm the air. Then again, perhaps they did not quite want to let go of them. Perhaps they swept them, and themselves, up and away in such haste so they could snatch one last look of love at their treasured possessions before locking them away for good, hammering them into the ground. Another claim of sorts. Where would all my friends be, where would their great, open-hearted, generous love of me be, without their fears?

A little later each morning a troop of laundry girls arrive from the village to bathe, taking their light relief early before the onset of the working day. They dive shrieking into the water, heads bobbing up and down, smashing their hands on to its surface to drive the foam into each other's faces, howling with mock protest as the drops run down over their noses and mouths before dripping back into the flow. The mist has vanished so the river now lies bare and ready to the eye. But the season has its own pace which somehow or other seems to have escaped them – not flustered and excited, but steady and quiet and slow. For a good while they do not see me. Almost immobile, I have been sitting reading on the bank in the shade of a tree. But then, as if sensing an observer, not quite an intruder, not some man loping around in the bushes and pretending he isn't there or that he is merely admiring the foliage, they hold still in the water, raise their eyes and, with a rush of awareness half-vexed, half-gratified, one by one they return my stare.

One of them has been coming to collect and leave the laundry at my aunt's villa every day. Sometimes I watch her from the upstairs window which looks over the back path as she approaches, always at the same time in the early afternoon, when everything inside the villa, resting to revive the hours ahead, goes quiet and dull and tired. She moves with the ease of someone who never has to think of how to dispose of her own time, someone whose mind has taken flight from what is asked of her body by the hour. She can worry freely at her life and loves, scale peaks, cross fjords, or simply dip herself in and out of the river as she walks. Her basket is full of my most intimate belongings, little luxury items of silk and satin and lace from my other life which I made sure to steal away. Apart from a lover, only a laundry girl is allowed to get this close, to sniff out a body till all its snobbery and decorum has gone. Since we have already been this far, she can afford, surely, the proper disrespect. After all, she has as good as touched me.

Before letting herself in through the door, she always shifts her basket from one hip to the other, tucks her hair round her ears, and then pushes the few strands that have fallen down over her forehead back under her cap. She has a glow which starts a little too high up on her cheeks. Not the complexion of a country girl, nor the rising heat of the day, but the flush of someone who, knowing how to hoard her most recent pleasures, and ready for the next chance, is more than happy to display them on her face. On about the third day I slip out of my room to meet her halfway down the stairs. Putting out my hand to take her basket, I squeeze and then, seeing that I am provoking no alarm, pinch, gently digging my nails into her arm.

Down by the river, after sporting in the water, the girls take off to the far bank. Although the sun is barely equal to the task at such an hour and such a season, they stretch themselves out to dry. Their bath robes, crumpled across their shoulders and under their backs, hang open over their legs, their swimming costumes gleaming with drops of moistness like tiny cuttings taken from the plump, translucent body of a jelly fish. They hardly stir except now and then to shift position, lifting a wet limb up from one spot on their robe and placing it down again on another, or turning over on to their stomachs or on to their sides. Dealing out the dampness nonchalantly as if it were a pack of cards. Their mood is as subdued now as it was elated just moments before. From where I am sitting they look like mildly agitated sleepers, troubled by some idle, not too pressing, physical discomfort such as hunger or thirst. I step into the water and wade over to the other side. Once inside the group their minimal gestures spring to life. They stir their legs and arms, holding them aloft only for as long as it takes to decide how – on whose body and where – to let them fall. Poised, like the arched neck of a swan getting ready to strike.

Down by the river, although there is shade, it is never dark. The light which bounces off the water is bluey green from the leaves overhead, which seem to have dropped in shreds under the surface. At the slightest agitation, the pieces start swimming around in the current like a school of fish slapping their tails and shoving each other aside in pursuit of the same piece of bait. On this side the bank is uneven, marked with pockets and dells where, should you want to although there is no need, you can hide. My laundry girl nudges me down a slope so that we are partly covered from sight. Nobody was looking. Nobody, that is, until a few moments ago, but me. Now I am part of the scene. By letting me into the group, they have shut down too bright a light and taken the harsh stare out of the sky. They have closed over me fiercely, like an eddy sucking a stone down fast to the river bed. My laundry girl smells of crimped and folded shirts. She smells of lace threaded through tiny metal holes still warm from the heating iron. She smells of me. I lie there almost completely still while she slides and scrapes down my side. Whether I like it or not and however much I like it, every caress and stroke has been procured. But even though it can only be a pretence, in the brief lull of the morning, these girls – my new clan we might say – have allowed me to drop sheer away from a world and class, my aunt's, his, to which I will never know – will it matter in the end? – if I ever really belonged.

By mid-morning the warmth of the day has almost reached its height. Then, after one final burst, the sun seems suddenly to empty out and lose all colour, dragging you from summer to autumn in the space of a few hours. Because the river is partly shaded, a chill comes over the water. No one else is around. The laundry girls have all trooped off to work, taking the edge off the afternoon. I lie on the bank feeling the heat drain away, noticing where the green has thinned from the leaves, where some of them have gone dry, creased and fallen already, receiving no flood of red or burnt yellow to hold them a little longer in their place. I have never been here in the winter so I have to imagine the trees stripped and the river, rushing faster, suddenly bared on every side. Then where do they go in the early hours of the morning? Where, before its burdens are upon them, do they meet to unclutter their day? I have become a child of the season. I will never stay inside a house, never turn into someone else's creature, slug of their dark indoors, again. I have not reached very far, lifted myself very high, just yet. But, if needs be, I would rather crawl around the depths of my own river bed.

At the back of my aunt's villa, on the other side where the land is flat, there are outhouses and a stable. Beyond them is a meadow fenced in by low bushes except at the far end, where it meets a run of elm trees. My aunt keeps only one horse, although she likes the stables to be properly tended so that at least her property can benefit from a standing which she herself will never enjoy. Her solitary mare occupies the furthest stall, its dense black coat so brushed and shiny that, with every move of its haunches or flick of its tail, it glows – strangely since you would expect such darkness to suck back every smallest hint of its own light. When I wander over to this part of the villa, there is nearly always a stable boy – he can't be much more than fourteen or fifteen – perfectly decked out in leather cap, green trousers tucked into his boots, and a red waistcoat. I don't know if he is aware of how few people come to the house, apart from the laundry girl, just the cook and one other servant who live there all the time. They go steadily about their business. But although nothing is declining or in disarray, no cracks in the wainscoting, no damp around the floorboards, no dull dark stain over the fire, the villa feels to me as if it has foreknowledge of some impending disaster. Or as if it is already living the time, perhaps as far as a century away, when it will start, slowly with no hand upon it, to fall into disrepair. Isolated in their outback, the stable boy and his horse stand proudly, a little conspiracy of the groomed. As he mucks out the stable, fetches hay and brushes down the mare, he talks to her very softly, patting, stroking and hushing – 'There there, don't you worry' – as if she were in pain, even though she makes no sound.

I cannot quite remember, but I think when still a child I once rode a horse. I have an image of me clutching its mane with my eyes almost shut, arms pressed into the side of its huge head, my chest flat against its neck, ankles rigid with fear, legs all out of rhythm rubbing its flanks the wrong way, and my feet pointing absurdly into the oncoming rush of air, while someone is shouting at me to sit up, give her some rein, be bold.

While I stand there chatting idly to the groom, he asks me if I would like, as he puts it, to give her a turn. He looks at me a little suspiciously. Perhaps he knows what goes on over the other side down by the river in the late mornings. Perhaps one of the laundry girls is his girl and lies with him later in the evening telling him all about me, pretending to have caught me out – nothing in it for her, of course – with one of her friends. He seems to sense that I am somewhat at a loss and scratches his head while we talk, as if there were some puzzle or mystery about our surroundings which it is up to the two of us to solve. I don't fit here. It is why I love the place. Of course I am a bit of an oddity, sticking out in the city finery, which I still front and cling to. But nothing quite fits here. Certainly not my aunt, who arrived in a big hurry to check on me right at the beginning and then realising there was nothing to be got out of me – all profit bled from her investment and no conversation – and that I seemed set to stay, just as quickly left. My aunt's villa is like one of those toy theatres made of cut-out bits of cardboard, sets and players alike, which don't join up properly so that as soon as you fasten a section together, some prop or a costume you adjusted only moments ago immediately comes away in your hands. Enough to make a child rave. Unless she suddenly decides to fling them about, not in a tantrum but for the sheer joy of it, and then watch to see what shapes and patterns they make as they slowly flutter back down.

'Go on,' he says. 'I'll have her saddled up in no time.' His voice is half coaxing, half gruff. Her sole charioteer. He shuffles from one foot to the other. Restive. Almost pawing the ground, while she stands there, not a twitch or shudder, perfectly silent and still. 'You'll soon get the hang of it.' He is testing me. Willing her, I am certain, to be unruly under his breath. I don't think he believes for a second that I will say yes.

As he legs me up, Octave, the chauffeur, all of them handing me into a motorcar flash before my eyes. Gallants guiding me, courtesy of their attention and a lost wallflower without them, on to the ballroom floor. I see them, chins up, eyes fixed on the ceiling, stepping from one foot to the other, pulling my arm above our heads and gently twisting it like the multi-coloured ribbon of a maypole. The stable boy puts his hand under the sole of my foot and shunts me up. I feel my legs spread to the limit – for a second I have my head down over her neck and one leg pointed behind me in the air like a frozen dancer – and then the sharp pull between my thighs before I bring my body down to nest, hugging, across hers.

I think the stable boy has understood that, while we may have started this together, we go no further, not he and I at least. His forehead is puckered, although the bottom half of his face is smiling, like an encouraging parent trying to hide their slowly building panic from their child and from themselves. He wipes his handkerchief across his brow. A terrible error. But there was no stopping her, she would have a go, he lies. He is already shaking his head. As he rehearses his story, I can see him fretting. Is it me or his beloved mare that he is betraying? Which one of us is he so covetously and recklessly, beyond all bounds of duty, letting go? He is covering his tracks all the more keenly because, unlike the rest of them, he can see – in his mind's eye we are already racing – that soon he will no longer be able to cover mine. What could be worse – worse for him, worse for the whole lot of them – than if I didn't fall? Perish the thought. I slip my feet through the stirrups and, pulling her head round, point her towards the meadow. She pricks her ears, pulls for a moment, then I feel the pressure slacken all down my arms. The sun stares straight into my eyes so I can see almost nothing in front of me, just the purple of the autumn harebells flecking the grass as they melt and blend into the sky.

She starts at the slowest canter, making a berth of the meadow, keeping to the edges along the fencing where the ground drops away at the other side, brushing past the elms which stand at the far end, lofty barriers with their heads in the clouds. Then, bit by bit, she starts to pick up speed. Her body flat out, turning back on her path in ever-diminishing circles as she pulls closer and closer to the centre. Each time she goes the rounds, the grass bends to her current, flattens, then lifts and swirls leaving rings of pale green in her wake that bruise and dent the earth like the vortex after an aeroplane has beaten its way off the ground. I hold on to her fast, sniffing the air, every pore dilating, my thighs slapped to her haunches. So fast does she propel herself that her legs are almost bent double underneath her, and her hooves almost strike her belly. She throws her bulk ahead of her, as if she would make it weightless. We are light and buoyant and empty as a balloon. Here is substance only to the blind, the dazed onlooker who fears for the rider like a child gasping at the man on the trapeze, never steadier than when he pretends to fall. The stable boy has gone, slouched away guilty, already muttering his defence. Had he stayed and watched, he would have felt the pull of the air rushing past him where he stood. Then he might have realised that the one at risk is the one who, refusing to bend or yield, hardens himself to the wind. Unerring my horse comes to a halt at the dead centre of the meadow, and rears herself up into the sun. We have spun ourselves into nothing. If I fall there will be no impact, no danger, there will be no fall at all. Danger only comes, I can see his pale face and his dark eyes widening with disbelief as I say it, to those who choose to stay behind.

Grateful acknowledgement to Céleste Albaret, *Monsieur Proust*, (1973), Robert Laffont; Simone Hoog and Daniel Meyer, *Versailles – Complete Guide*, (2000), Edition Art Lys; and Rachel Bowlby, *Just Looking – Consumer culture in Dreiser, Gissing and Zola*, (1985), Methuen.